Frederick The Great And His Family

A Historical Novel
Book I

by

L. Mühlbach

ABOUT THE AUTHOR

Luise Muhlbach, born Clara Maria Regina Muller on January 2, 1814, in Neubrandenburg, Germany, was a renowned German writer acclaimed for her historical fiction. Writing under the pseudonym Luise Muhlbach, she captivated readers with vivid narratives that brought history to life. Despite a relatively short-lived period of popularity, her works continue to resonate with audiences. Born to Friedrich Andreas Müller and Friederika Müller (nee Strübing), Clara displayed early literary talent that flourished into a prolific career. Her most famous novel, "Frederick the Great and His Court" (German: Friedrich der Grosse und sein Hof), stands as a testament to her narrative prowess. This and many other works were translated into English, broadening her reach and influence. Muhlbach's storytelling skill lay in her ability to intertwine historical accuracy with compelling characters and plotlines, transporting readers to different epochs with ease. Through her writing, she illuminated the complexities of bygone eras, offering insights into the lives of prominent figures and the societies they inhabited. Though she passed away on September 26, 1873, in Berlin, Muhlbach's literary legacy endures, ensuring that her contributions to the genre of historical fiction remain cherished and celebrated by generations of readers worldwide.

CONTENTS

CHAPTER I
THE KING

The king laid his flute aside, and with his hands folded behind his back, walked thoughtfully up and down his room in Sans-Souci. His countenance was now tranquil, his brow cloudless; with the aid of music he had harmonized his soul, and the anger and displeasure he had so shortly before felt were soothed by the melodious notes of his flute.

The king was no longer angry, but melancholy, and the smile that played on his lip was so resigned and painful that the brave Marquis d'Argens would have wept had he seen it, and the stinging jest of Voltaire have been silenced.

But neither the marquis nor Voltaire, nor any of his friends were at present in Potsdam. D'Argens was in France, with his young wife, Barbe Cochois; Voltaire, after a succession of difficulties and quarrels, had departed forever; General Rothenberg had also departed to a land from which no one returns—he was dead! My lord marshal had returned to Scotland, Algarotti to Italy, and Bastiani still held his office in Breslau. Sans-Souci, that had been heretofore the seat of joy and laughing wit—Sans-Souci was now still and lonely; youth, beauty, and gladness had forsaken it forever; earnestness and duty had taken their place, and reigned in majesty within those walls that had so often echoed with the happy laugh and sparkling jest of the king's friends and contemporaries.

Frederick thought of this, as with folded hands he walked up and down, and recalled the past. Sunk in deep thought, he remained standing before a picture that hung on the wall above his secretary, which represented Barbarina in the fascinating costume of a shepherdess, as he had seen her for the first time ten years ago; it had been painted by Pesne for the king. What recollections, what dreams arose before the king's soul as he gazed at that bewitching and lovely face; at those soft, melting eyes, whose glance had once made him so happy! But that was long ago; it had passed like a sunbeam on a rainy day, it had been long buried in clouds. These remembrances warmed the king's heart as he now stood so solitary and loveless before this picture; and he confessed to that sweet image, once so fondly loved, what he had never admitted to himself, that his heart was very lonely.

But these painful recollections, these sad thoughts, did not last. The king roused himself from those dangerous dreams, and on leaving the picture cast upon it almost a look of hatred.

"This is folly," he said; "I will to work."

He approached the secretary, and seized the sealed letters and packets that were lying there. "A letter and packet from the queen," he said, wonderingly opening the letter first. Casting a hasty glance through it, a mocking smile crossed his face. "She sends me a French translation of a prayer-book," he said, shrugging his shoulders. "Poor queen! her heart is not yet dead, though, by Heaven! it has suffered enough."

He threw the letter carelessly aside, without glancing at the book; its sad, pleading prayer was but an echo of the thoughts trembling in her heart.

"Bagatelles! nothing more," he murmured, after reading the other letters and laying them aside. He then rang hastily, and bade the servant send Baron Pollnitz to him as soon as he appeared in the audience-chamber.

A few minutes later the door opened, and the old, wrinkled, sweetly smiling face of the undaunted courtier appeared.

"Approach," said the king, advancing a few steps to meet him. "Do you bring me his submission? Does my brother Henry acknowledge that it is vain to defy my power?"

Pollnitz shrugged his shoulders. "Sire," he said, sighing, "his highness will not understand that a prince must have no heart. He still continues in his disobedience, and declares that no man should marry a woman without loving her; that he would be contemptible and cowardly to allow himself to be forced to do what should be the free choice of his own heart."

Pollnitz had spoken with downcast eyes and respectful countenance; he appeared not to notice that the king reddened and his eyes burned with anger.

"Ah! my brother dared to say that?" cried the king. "He has the Utopian thought to believe that he can defy my wishes. Tell him he is mistaken; he must submit to me as I had to submit to my father."

"He gives that as an example why he will not yield. He believes a forced marriage can never be a happy one; that your majesty had not only made yourself unhappy by your marriage, but also your queen, and that there was not a lady in the land who would exchange places with your wife."

The king glanced piercingly at Pollnitz. "Do you know it would have been better had you forgotten a few of my wise brother's words?"

"Your majesty commanded me to tell you faithfully every word the prince said."

"And you are too much a man of truth and obedience, too little of a courtier, not to be frank and faithful. Is it not so? Ah! vraiment, I know you, and I know very well that you are playing a double game. But I warn you not to follow the promptings of your wicked heart. I desire my brother to marry, do you hear? I will it, and you, the grand chamberlain, Baron Pollnitz, shall feel my anger if he does not consent."

"And if he does?" said Pollnitz, in his laughing, shameless manner; "if I persuade the prince to submit to your wishes, what recompense shall I receive?"

"On the day of their betrothal, I will raise your income five hundred crowns, and pay your debts."

"Ah, sire, in what a pitiable dilemma you are placing me! Your majesty wishes Prince Henry to engage himself as soon as possible, and I must now wish it to be as late as possible."

"And why?"

"Because I must hasten to make as many debts as possible, that your majesty may pay them."

"You are and will remain an unmitigated fool; old age will not even cure you," said the king, smiling. "But speak, do you think my brother may be brought to reason?"

Pollnitz shrugged his shoulders, gave a sly smile, but was silent.

"You do not answer me. Is my brother in love? and has he confided in you?"

"Sire, I believe the prince is in love from ennui alone, but he swears it is his first love."

"That is an oath that is repeated to each lady-love; I am not afraid of it," said the king, smiling "Who is the enchantress that has heard his first loving vows? She is doubtless a fairy—a goddess of beauty."

"Yes, sire, she is young and beautiful, and declares it is also her first love, so no one can doubt its purity; no one understands love as well as this fair lady; no other than Madame von Kleist, who, as your majesty remembers, was lately divorced from her husband."

"And is now free to love again, as it appears," said the king, with a mocking smile. "But the beautiful Louise von Schwerin is a dangerous, daring woman, and we must check her clever plans in the bud. If she desires to be loved by my brother, she possesses knowledge, beauty, and experience to gain her point and to lead him into all manner of follies. This affair must be brought quickly to a close, and Prince Henry acknowledged to be the prince royal."

"Prince Henry goes this evening to Berlin to attend a feast given by the Prince of Prussia," whispered Pollnitz.

"Ah! it is true the prince's arrest ceases at six o'clock, but he will not forget that he needs permission to leave Potsdam."

"He will forget it, sire."

The king walked up and down in silence, and his countenance assumed an angry and threatening appearance. "This struggle must be brought to a close, and that speedily. My brother must submit to my authority. Go and watch his movements; as soon as he leaves, come to me."

Long after Pollnitz had left him, the king paced his chamber in deep thought. "Poor Henry! I dare not sympathize with you; you are a king's son—that means a slave to your position. Why has Providence given hearts to kings as to other men? Why do we thirst so for love? as the intoxicating drink is always denied us, and we dare not drink it even when offered by the most bewitching enchantress!"

Involuntarily his eye rested upon the beautiful picture of Barbarina. But he would have no pity with himself, as he dared not show mercy to his brother. Seizing the silver bell, he rang it hastily.

"Take that picture from the wall, and carry it immediately to the inspector, and tell him to hang it in the picture-gallery," said Frederick.

He looked on quietly as the servant took the picture down and carried it from the room, then sighed and gazed long at the plane where it had hung.

"Empty and cold! The last token of my youth is gone! I am now the king, and, with God's blessing, will be the father of my people."

CHAPTER II
PRINCE HENRY

Prince Henry sat quiet and motionless in his lonely room; dark thoughts seemed to trouble him; his brow was clouded, his lips compressed. Had you not known him, you would have taken him for the king, so great was the resemblance of the two brothers; but it was only an outward resemblance. The prince had not the spiritual expression, his eyes had not the passionate fire, his face (beautiful as it was) wanted the fascinating geniality, the sparkling inspiration, that at all times lighted the king's countenance like a sunbeam.

The prince possessed a greater mind, a clearer understanding, but he wanted soul and poetic feeling, and allowed himself at times to ridicule his brother's poetic efforts. The king, knowing this, was inclined to regard the shortcomings of the prince as a determined contempt and resistance to his command; and as the prince became more reckless and more indifferent, he became more severe and harsh. Thus the struggle commenced that had existed for some time between the two brothers.

For the last four days the prince had been in arrest for disobeying orders, but the hour of his release was approaching, and he awaited it with impatience.

The bell of the nearest church had just announced the hour of six. The door opened immediately, and an officer, in the name of the king, pronounced his arrest at an end.

The prince answered with a low bow, and remained seated, pointing haughtily to the door; but as the officer left him he arose and paced hastily to and fro.

"He treats me like a school-boy," he murmured; "but I shall show him that I have a will of my own! I will not be intimidated—I will not submit; and if the king does not cease to annoy me, if he continues to forget that I am not a slave, but son and brother of a king, no motives shall restrain me, and I also will forget, as he does, that I am a prince, and remember only that I am a free, responsible man. He wishes me to marry, and therefore has me followed, and surrounds me with spies. He wishes to force me to marry. Well, I will marry, but I will choose my own wife!"

The prince had just made this resolve, when the door opened, and the servant announced that Messrs. Kalkreuth and Kaphengst awaited his commands.

He bade them enter, and advancing smilingly gave them his hand.

"Welcome! welcome!" he said; "the cage is open, and I may enjoy a little air and sunshine; let us not delay to make use of this opportunity. Our horses shall be saddled."

"They are already saddled, prince," said Baron Kalkreuth. "I have ordered them to the court, and as soon as it is dark we will mount them."

"What! is it not best that we should mount before my door and ride openly away?" said the prince, wonderingly.

"It is my opinion that is the best plan," cried Baron Kaphengst, laughing gayly. "Every one will believe your highness to be simply taking a ride, while curiosity would be raised if we left the city on foot."

"I think leaving in the dark, and on foot, looks as if I were afraid," said the prince, thoughtfully.

"Secrecy is good for priests and old women, but not for us," cried Kaphengst.

"Secrecy suits all who wish to do wrong," said Kalkreuth, earnestly.

The prince glanced hastily at him. "You believe, then, we are about to do wrong?"

"I dare not speak of your highness, but we two are certainly doing wrong; we are about to commit an act of insubordination. But still, my prince, I am ready to do so, as your highness wishes us to accompany you."

The prince did not answer, but stepped to the window, and looked out thoughtfully and silently. In a few moments he returned, looking calm and resolute.

"Kalkreuth is right—we were going to do wrong, and we must avoid it. I shall write to the king, and ask leave for you and myself to go to Berlin."

"That is, unfortunately, impossible," said a sweet voice behind him, and as the prince turned he saw the smiling face of Pollnitz. "I beg pardon, your highness, for having entered unannounced, but you allowed me to come at this hour and give you an account of the commissions you gave me."

"Why do you say it is impossible to obtain leave of the king today?" asked Henry, hastily.

"Because his majesty is already in the concert-saloon, and your highness knows that he has strictly forbidden any one to disturb him there."

"We shall, then, have to give up our plan and remain here," said the prince.

Kaphengst glanced angrily and threateningly at his friend.

"And why should your highness do this?" asked Pollnitz, astonished. "All your preparations are made, all your commands fulfilled. I have procured your costumes; no one will recognize you, and if they should, would not dare to betray you to the king. Only two persons know that you are to visit the ball, the Prince of Prussia, and a lovely lady, whose beautiful eyes were misty with tears when I delivered her your message. 'Tell the prince,' she murmured, in a tender voice, 'I will await him there, even if I knew the king would crush me with his anger.'"

The prince blushed with joy. "And you say it is impossible for me to see the king?"

"Impossible, my prince."

"Well, we will have to renounce it," said the prince, sighing.

"Renounce seeing the king, yes! for he will not leave his rooms in Sans-Souci today."

"Then we would be entirely safe; he would not notice our departure," said Kaphengst, quickly.

"Entirely safe," said Pollnitz.

"That is, if Baron Pollnitz does not himself inform the king," said Baron Kalkreuth, whose quick, clear glance rested upon the smiling face of the courtier, and appeared to read his inmost thoughts.

Baron Pollnitz cast a suspicious and angry glance at Kalkreuth. "I did not know that borrowing money from you gave you the right to speak rudely to me!"

"Silence! gentlemen," cried the prince, who, until now, had stood quietly struggling with his own wishes. "Take your cloaks and let us walk. Did you not say that horses were awaiting us at the door, Baron Kalkreuth?"

"I said so, your highness."

"And you Pollnitz? Did you not say that three costumes awaited us in Berlin?"

"Yes, your highness."

"Well, then," said the prince, smiling, "we must not allow the horses and costumes to await us any longer. Come, gentlemen, we will ride to Berlin."

"Really it was hard to get him off," murmured Pollnitz, as he regained the street, and saw the three young men fading in the distance. "The good prince had quite a dutiful emotion; if the king only knew it, he would forgive him all, and renounce the idea of his marriage. But that would not suit me—my debts would not be paid! I must not tell the king of his brother's inward struggle."

"Well!" said the king, as Pollnitz entered, "has my brother really gone to Berlin?"

"Yes, your majesty, and accompanied by the two Messieurs—"

"Silence!" cried the king, hastily; "I do not wish to know their names, I should have to punish them also. He has then gone, and without any hesitation, any reluctance?"

"Yes, sire, without hesitation. He thinks he has the right to go where he pleases, and to amuse himself as he can."

"Order the carriage, Pollnitz," said the king. "Without doubt my brother has taken the shortest road to Berlin?"

"Yes, sire."

"Then there is no danger of our meeting them and being recognized; and as we have relays on the road, we will reach Berlin before them."

CHAPTER III
LOUISE VON KLEIST

Madame von Kleist was alone in her boudoir. She had just completed her toilet, and was viewing herself with considerable pleasure in a large Venetian glass. She had reason to be pleased. The costume of an odalisque became her wonderfully; suited her luxuriant beauty, her large, dreamy blue eyes, her full red lips, her slender, swaying form. At twenty-eight, Louise von Kleist was still a sparkling beauty; the many trials and sorrows she had passed through had not scattered the roses from her cheek, nor banished youth from her heart.

Louise von Kleist resembled greatly the little Louise von Schwerin of earlier days—the little dreamer who found it romantic to love a gardener, and was quite ready to flee with him to a paradise of love. The king's watchfulness saved her from this romantic folly, and gave her another husband. This unhappy match was now at an end. Louise was again free. She still felt in her heart some of the wild love of romance and adventure of the little Louise; she was the same daring, dreamy, impressible Louise, only now she was less innocent. The little coquette from instinct was changed into a coquette from knowledge.

She stood before the glass and surveyed once more her appearance; then acknowledged with a pleased smile that she was beautiful enough to fascinate all men, to arouse in all hearts a painful longing.

"But I shall love no one but the prince," she said, "and when my power over him is sufficient to induce him to marry me, I shall reward him by my faith, and entire submission to his wishes. Oh! I shall be a virtuous wife, a true and faithful mother; and my lovely little Camilla shall find in her mother a good and noble example. I shall promise this to my angel with my farewell kiss; and then—to the ball!"

She entered the next chamber, and stood at her child's bed. What a strange sight! This woman, in a fantastic, luxuriant costume, bending over the cot of the little girl, with such tender, pious looks, with folded hands, and soft, murmuring lips, uttering a prayer or holy wish!

"How beautiful she is!" murmured Louise, not dreaming that her own beauty at this moment beamed with touching splendor—that mother love had changed the alluring coquette into an adorable saint—"how beautiful she is!"

The gay, ringing laughter of her daughter interrupted her; the child opened her large black eyes, and looked amused.

"You naughty child, you were not asleep," said Louise.

"No, mamma, I was not asleep; I was playing comedy."

"Ah! and who taught you to play comedy, you silly child?" said Louise, tenderly.

The child looked earnestly before her for a few moments as children are wont to do when a question surprises them.

"I believe, mamma," she said, slowly—"I believe I learned it from you."

"From me, Camilla? When have you seen me act?"

"Oh, very often," she cried, laughing. "Just a few days ago, mamma, don't you remember when we were laughing and talking so merrily together, Prince Henry was announced, and you sent me into the next room, but the door was open, and I saw very well that you made a sad face, and I heard the prince ask you how you were, and you answered, 'I am sick, your highness, and how could it be otherwise, as I am always sad or weeping?' Now, mother, was not that acting?"

Louise did not answer. Breathing heavily, she laid her hand upon her heart, for she felt a strange sorrow and indescribable fear.

Camilla continued, "Oh! and I saw how tenderly the prince looked at you; how he kissed you, and said you were as lovely as an angel. Oh, mamma, I too shall be beautiful, and beloved by a prince!"

"To be beautiful, darling, you must be good and virtuous," said the fair odalisque, earnestly.

Little Camilla arose in her bed; the white gown fell from her shoulders and exposed her soft childish form, her brown ringlets curled down her neck and lost themselves in her lace-covered dress.

The chandelier that hung from the ceiling lighted her lovely face, and made the gold and silver embroidered robes and jewels of her mother sparkle brilliantly.

At this moment, as with folded arms she glanced up at her mother, she looked like an angel, but she had already dangerous and earthly thoughts in her heart.

"Mamma," she said, "why should I be virtuous, when you are not?"

Louise trembled, and looked terrified at her daughter. "Who told you I was not virtuous?"

"My poor, dear papa told me when he was here the last time. Oh, he told me a great deal, mamma! He told," continued the child, with a sly smile, "how you loved a beautiful gardener, and ran off with him, and how he, at the command of the king, married you and saved you from shame; and he said you were not at all grateful, but had often betrayed and deceived him, and, because he was so unhappy with you, he drank so much wine to forget his sorrow. Oh, mamma, you don't know how poor papa cried as he told me all this, and besought me not to become like you, but to be good, that every one might love and respect me!"

Whilst Camilla spoke, her mother had sunk slowly, as if crushed, to the floor; and, with her face buried in the child's bed, sobbed aloud.

"Don't cry, mamma," said Camilla, pleadingly; "believe me, I will not do as papa says, and I will not be so stupid as to live in a small town, where it is so still and lonesome."

As her mother still wept, Camilla continued, as if to quiet her:

"I shall be like you, mamma; indeed, I will. Oh, you should but see how I watch you, and notice how you smile at all the gentlemen, what soft eyes you make, and then again, how cold and proud you are, and then look at them so tenderly! Oh, I have noticed all, and I shall do just the same, and I will run away with a gardener, but I will not let papa catch me—no, not I."

"Hush, child, hush!" cried the mother, rising, pale and trembling, from her knees; "you must become a good and virtuous girl, and never run away with a man. Forget what your bad father has told you; you know he hates me, and has told you all these falsehoods to make you do the same."

"Mamma, can you swear that it is not true?"

"Yes, my child, I can swear it."

"You did not run off with a gardener?"

"No, my child. Have I not told you that a virtuous girl never runs away?"

"You did not make papa unhappy, and, being his wife, love other men?"

"No, my daughter."

"Mamma," said the child, after a long pause, "can you give me your right hand, and swear you did not?"

Louise hesitated a moment; a cold shiver ran through her, she felt as if she was about to perjure herself; but as she looked into the beautiful face of her child, whose eyes were fixed on her with a strange expression, she overcame her unwillingness.

"Here is my hand—I swear that all your father told you is false!"

Camilla laughed gleefully. "Oh, mamma, I have caught you: you always want me to tell the truth, and never give my right hand when a thing is not true, and now you have done it yourself."

"What have I done!" said the mother, trembling.

"You gave me your right hand, and swore that all papa told me was false; and I say it is true, and you have sworn falsely."

"Why do you believe that, Camilla?" she asked.

"I don't believe it, I know it," said the child, with a sly smile, "When papa spoke to you, for the last time, and told you good-by forever, he told you the same he had told me. Oh! I was there and heard all; you did not see me slip into the room and hide behind the fire-place. Papa told you that you had been the cause of all his unhappiness and shame; that from the day you had run off with the gardener and he, at the king's command, went after you, and married you—from that day, he had been a lost man, and when he said that, you cried, but did not tell him, as you told me, that it was not true."

Louise did not answer. This last taunt had crushed her heart, and silenced her. Still leaning on the bed, she looked at her child with painful tenderness. Camilla's mocking laughter had pierced her soul as with a dagger.

"Lost," she murmured, "both of us lost!"

With passionate despair she threw her arms around the child, and pressed her closely; kissed her wildly again and again, and covered her face with burning tears.

"No, Camilla, no! you shall not be lost, you must remain good and pure! Every child has its guardian angel; pray, my child, pray that your angel may watch over you!"

She pressed her again in her arms, then returned to her chamber, sadder and more hopeless than she had ever been before.

But this unusual sadness commenced to annoy her; her heart was not accustomed to feel sorrow, and her remorseful, dreary feeling made her shudder. "If the carriage would but come!" she murmured, and then, as if to excuse her thoughtlessness, she added, "it is now my holy duty to listen to the prince; I must regain the respect of my child. Yes, yes, I must become the wife of Henry I I can accomplish this, for the prince loves me truly."

And now, she was again the coquette, whose captivating smile harmonized perfectly with her alluring costume—no longer the tender mother, no longer the sinner suffering from repentance and self-reproach.

She stood before the glass, and arranged her disordered dress and smoothed her dishevelled hair.

"I must be bewitching and fascinating," she murmured, with a smile that showed two rows of pearl-like teeth; "the prince must gain courage from my glance, to offer me his hand. Oh, I know he is quite prepared to do so, if it were only to annoy his brother!" As she saw the carriage drive up, she exclaimed, with sparkling eyes, "The battle begins—to victory!"

CHAPTER IV
AT THE MASKED BALL

The feast had commenced. As Louise von Kleist, the beautiful odalisque, entered the dancing-saloon, she was almost blinded by the gay and sparkling assembly. The fairy-like and fantastic robes sparkled with gold and jewels. The sea of light thrown from the crystal chandelier upon the mirrors and ornaments of the brilliant saloon dazzled the eye. The entertainments of the Prince of Prussia were renowned for their taste and splendor.

Unrecognized, the beautiful Louise slipped through the gay assembly of masks, and, when detecting some friends under the muffled forms of their disguise, she murmured their names, and some mischievous and witty remark; then springing gayly on to shoot again her arrow, and excite astonishment and surprise.

"Oh, that life were a masked ball!" she murmured softly to herself, "mysterious and sweet! where you find more than you seek, and guess more than is known. No one recognizes me here. The brave and handsome Count Troussel, who is leaning against that pillar, and casting such melancholy glances through the crowd, hunting for the one his heart adores, never dreams that she is standing opposite him, and is laughing at his perplexity. No, he does not recognize me, and no one knows my costume but the prince and Pollnitz, and as they have not yet found me, I conclude they have not arrived. I will therefore amuse myself during their absence."

She was just approaching the sentimental cavalier, when she suddenly felt her arm touched, and, turning around, saw two masks wrapped in dark dominoes before her.

"Beautiful odalisque, I bring you your sultan." murmured one of them, in whom she recognized Baron Pollnitz.

"And where is my sultan?" she asked.

"Here," said the second mask, offering the beautiful lady his arm. Louise saw those glorious eyes beaming upon her through his mask-eyes which the king and Prince Henry alone possessed.

"Ah, my prince!" she murmured softly and reproachfully, "you see that it is I who have waited."

The prince did not answer, but conducted her hastily through the crowd. They had soon reached the end of the saloon. A small flight of steps led them to a little boudoir opening on a balcony. Into this boudoir Pollnitz led the silent pair, then bowing low he left them.

"My God! your highness, if we should be surprised here!"

"Fear nothing, we will not be surprised. Pollnitz guards the door. Now, as we are alone and undisturbed, let us lay aside our disguises."

Thus speaking, the supposed prince removed his mask and laid it upon the table.

"The king!" cried Louise, terrified and stepping back.

The king's eyes rested upon her with a piercing glance. "What!" he asked, "are you still acting? You appear astonished; and still you must have known me. Who but the king would show the beautiful Madame von Kleist such an honor? In what other cavalier could you place such perfect confidence as to accompany him into this lonely boudoir? With whom but the king could you have trusted your fair fame? You need not be alarmed; to be in my presence is to be under my protection—the kind guardianship of your king. I thank you that you knew me, and, knowing me, followed me trustingly."

The searching glance of the king alarmed Louise; his mocking words bewildered her, and she was incapable of reply.

She bowed silently, and allowed herself to be conducted to the divan.

"Sit down, and let us chat awhile," said the king. "You know I hate the noise of a feast, and love to retire into some corner, unnoticed and unseen. I had no sooner discovered the fair Louise under this charming costume, than I knew I had found good company. I ordered Pollnitz to seek out for us some quiet spot, where we might converse freely. Commence, therefore."

"Of what shall I speak, your majesty?" said Louise, confused and frightened. She knew well that the king had not found her by chance, but had sought her with a determined purpose.

"Oh! that is a question whose naivete reminds me of the little Louise Schwerin of earlier days. Well, let us speak on that subject which interests most deeply all who know you; let us speak of your happiness. You sigh. Have you already paid your tribute? Do you realize the fleetness of all earthly bliss?"

"Ah! your majesty, an unhappy marriage is the most bitter offering that can be made to experience," sighed Madame von Kliest. "My life was indeed wretched until released by your kindness from that bondage."

"Ah, yes, it is true you are divorced. When and upon whom will you now bestow this small, white hand?"

Louise looked up astonished. "What!" she stammered, confused, "your majesty means—"

"That you will certainly marry again. As beautiful a lady as you will always be surrounded by lovers, and I sincerely hope that you will marry. You should go forward as an example to my brothers, your youthful playmates, and I will tell my brother Henry that marriage is not so bad a thing, as the beautiful Madame von Kleist has tried it for the second time."

"I doubt very much, sire," said Louise, timidly, "if the example of so insignificant a person would have the desired effect upon the prince."

"You do yourself injustice. The prince has too strong an admiration for you, not to be influenced by your encouraging example. My brother must and shall marry according to his birth. I am assured that, contrary to my wishes and commands, he is about to make a secret and illegitimate marriage. I am not yet acquainted with the name of his wily mistress, but I shall learn it, and, when once noted in my memory, woe be unto her, for I shall never acknowledge such a marriage, and I shall take care that his mistress is not received at court—she shall be regarded as a dishonored woman."

"Your majesty is very stern and pitiless toward the poor prince," said Madame Kleist, who had succeeded in suppressing her own emotions, and, following the lead of the king, she was desirous to let it appear that the subject was one of no personal interest to herself.

"No," said the king, "I am not cruel and not pitiless. I must forget that I am a brother, and remember only I am a king, not only for the good of my family, but for the prosperity of my people. My brother must marry a princess of wealth and influence. Tell Prince Henry this. Now," said the king, with an engaging smile, "let us speak of your lovely self. You will, of course, marry again. Have you not confidence enough in me to tell me the name of your happy and favored lover?"

"Sire," said Louise, smiling, "I do not know it myself, and to show what unbounded confidence I have in your majesty, I modestly confess that I am not positively certain whether among my many followers there is one who desires to be the successor of Kleist. It is easy to have many lovers, but somewhat difficult to marry suitably."

"We need a marrying man to chase away the crowd of lovers," said the king, smiling. "Think awhile—let your lovers pass in review before you—perhaps you may find among them one who is both ardent and desirable."

Louise remained thoughtful for a few moments. The king observed her closely.

"Well," he said, after a pause, "have you made your selection?"

Madame von Kleist sighed, and her beautiful bright eyes filled with tears. She took leave of her most cherished and ambitious dream—bade farewell to her future of regal pomp and splendor.

"Yes, sire, I have found an e'poitseur, who only needs encouragement, to offer me his heart and hand."

"Is he of good family?"

"Yes, sire."

"Military?"

"Yes, sire. He wears only a captain's epaulets. Your majesty sees that I am modest."

"On the day of his marriage he shall be major. When the Church pronounces her blessing, the king's blessing shall not be wanting. We are, of course, agreed. When will you be engaged?"

"Sire, that depends upon my lover, and when I succeed in bringing him to terms."

"We will say in eight days. You see I am anxious to become speedily acquainted with one blissful mortal, and I think that the husband of the beautiful Madame Kleist will be supremely happy. In eight days, then, you will be engaged, and, to complete your good work, you must announce this happy fact to my brother Henry. Of course, he must not even surmise that you sacrifice yourself in order to set him a good example. No, you will complete your noble work, and tell him that a love which you could not control induced you to take this step; and that he may not doubt your words, you will tell your story cheerfully—yes, joyously."

"Sire, it is too much—I cannot do it," cried Madame von Kleist. "It is enough to trample upon my own heart; your majesty cannot desire me to give the prince his death-blow."

The king's eyes flashed angrily, but he controlled himself.

"His death!" he repeated, shrugging his shoulders, "as if men died of such small wounds. You know better yourself. You know that the grave of one love is the cradle of another. Be wise, and do as I tell you: in eight days you will be engaged, and then you will have the kindness to acquaint Prince Henry with your happy prospects."

"Ah, sire, do not be so cruel as to ask this of me," cried Louise, gliding from the divan upon her knees, "be merciful. I am ready to obey the commands of my king, to make the sacrifice that is asked of me—let it not be too great a one. Your majesty asks that I shall draw down the contempt of the man I love upon myself; that this man must not only give me up, but scorn me. You require too much. This is more than the strongest, bravest heart can endure. Your majesty knows that the prince loves me passionately. Ah, sire, your brother would have forfeited his rank and your favor by marrying me, but he would have been a happy man; and I ask the king if that is not, at last, the best result? Are you, sire, content and happy since you trampled your breathing, loving heart to death at the foot of the throne? You command your brother to do as you have done. Well, sire, I submit—not only to resign the prince, but to marry again, to marry without love. Perhaps my soul will be lost by this perjury, but what matters that—it is a plaything in the hands of the king? He may break my heart, but it shall not be dishonored and trodden in the dust. The prince shall cease to love me, but I will not be despised by him. He shall not think me a miserable coquette, despise, and laugh at me. Now, sire, you can crush me in your anger. I have said what I had to say—you know my decision."

She bowed her head almost to the earth; motionless, kneeling at the foot of the king, her hands folded on her breast, she might in reality have been taken for an odalisque but that her sad, tearful face was not in unison with the situation or costume.

A long pause ensued—a solemn, fearful pause. The king struggled with his rage, Louise with her disappointment and distress. Sounds of laughter, the gay notes of music reached them from the dancing-saloon. The ball had commenced, and youth and beauty were mingling in the dance. These sounds aroused the king, and the sad contrast made Louise shudder.

"You will not, then, comply with my request?" said the king, sternly.

"Sire, I cannot!" murmured Louise, raising her hands imploringly to the king.

"You cannot!" cried the king, whose face glowed with anger; "you cannot, that means you will not, because your vain, coquettish heart will not resign the love of the prince. You submit to resign his hand, because you must; but you wish to retain his love: he must think of you as a heavenly ideal, to be adored and longed for, placed amongst the stars for worship. Ah, madame, you are not willing to make the gulf between you impassable! You say you wish, at least, to retain the respect of Prince Henry. I ask you, madame, what you have done to deserve his respect? You were an ungrateful and undutiful daughter; you did not think of the shame and sorrow you prepared for your parents, when you arranged your flight with the gardener. I succeeded in rescuing you from dishonor by marrying you to a brave and noble cavalier. It depended upon you entirely to gain his love and respect, but you forgot your duty as a wife, as you had forgotten it as a daughter. You had no pity with the faults and follies of your husband, you drove him to despair. At last, to drown his sorrows, he became a drunkard, and you, instead of remaining at his side to encourage and counsel him, deserted him, and so heartlessly exposed his shame that I, to put an end to the scandal, permitted your divorce. You not only forgot your duty as a wife and daughter, but also as a mother. You have deprived your child of a father, you have made her an orphan; you have soiled, almost depraved her young soul; and now, after all this, you wish to be adored and respected as a saint by my poor brother! No, madame! I shall know how to save him from this delusion; I shall tell to him and the world the history of little Louise von Schwerin! Fritz Wendel still lives, and, if you desire it, I can release him, and he may tell his romantic story."

"Oh, for the second time to-day I have heard that hateful name!" cried Louise; "the past is an avenger that pursues us mercilessly through our whole lives."

"Choose, madame!" said the king, after a pause; "will you announce your betrothal to my brother in a gay and unembarrassed tone, or shall I call Fritz Wendel, that he may sing the unhappy prince to sleep with his romantic history?"

Whilst the king spoke, Louise had raised herself slowly from her knees, and taken a seat upon the divan. Now rising, and bowing lowly, she said, with trembling lips and tearful voice: "Sire, I am prepared to do all that you wish. I shall announce my betrothal to the prince cheerfully, and without sighs or tears. But be merciful, and free me forever from that hideous spectre which seems ever at my side!"

"Do you mean poor Fritz Wendel?" said the king, smiling.

"Well, on the day of your marriage I will send him as a soldier to Poland: there he may relate his love-adventures, but no one will understand him. Are you content?"

"I thank you, sire," said Louise, faintly.

"Ah, I see our conversation has agitated you a little!" said the king. "Fortunately, we are now at an end. In the next eight days, remember, you will be engaged!"

"Yes, sire."

"The day of your marriage, I will make your captain a major. You promise to tell my brother of your engagement, and that it is in accordance with the warmest wishes of your heart?"

"Yes, sire; and you will banish the gardener forever?"

"I will; but wait—one thing more. Where will you tell my brother of your engagement, and before what witnesses?"

"At the place and before the witnesses your majesty may select," said Madame von Kleist.

The king thought a moment. "You will do it in my presence," said he; "I will let you know the time and place through Pollnitz. We have arranged our little affairs, madame, and we will descend to the saloon where, I think, your epouseur is sighing for your presence."

"Let him sigh, sire! With your permission, I should like to retire."

"Go, madame, where you wish. Pollnitz will conduct you to your carriage."

He offered her his hand, and, with a friendly bow, led her to the door.

"Farewell, madame! I believe we part friends?"

"Sire," she answered, smiling faintly, "I can only say as the soldiers do, 'I thank you for your gracious punishment!'"

She bowed and left the room hastily, that the king might not see her tears.

CHAPTER V
A SECRET CAPTAIN

The king looked long after her in silence; at first with an expression of deep pity, but this soon gave place to a gay, mocking smile.

"She is not a woman to take sorrow earnestly. When mourning no longer becomes her, she will lay it aside for the rosy robes of joy. She is a coquette, nothing more. It is useless to pity her."

He now stepped upon the balcony that overlooked the saloon, and glanced furtively from behind the curtains upon the gay assembly below.

"Poor, foolish mankind! how wise you might be, if you were not so very childish—if you did not seek joy and happiness precisely where it is not to be found! But how is this?" said the king, interrupting himself, "those two giant forms at the side of the little Armenians are certainly Barons Kalkreuth and Kaphengst, and that is my brother with them. Poor Henry! you have made a bad use of your freedom, and must, therefore, soon lose it. Ah! see how searchingly he turns his head, seeking his beautiful odalisque! In vain, my brother, in vain! For to-day, at least, we have made her a repentant Magdalen; to-morrow she will be again a life-enjoying Aspasia. Ah, the prince separates himself from his followers. I have a few words to whisper in the ear of the gay Kaphengst."

The king stepped back into the room, and after resuming his mask, he descended into the saloon, accompanied by his grand chamberlain.

Mirth and gayety reigned; the room was crowded with masks. Here stood a group in gay conversation; there was dancing at the other end of the saloon. Some were listening to the organ-player, as he sang, in comical German and French verses, little incidents and adventures that had occurred during the present year at court, bringing forth laughter, confused silence, and blushes. Some were amusing themselves with the lively, witty chat of the son of the Prince of Prussia, the little ten-year-old, Prince Frederick William. He was dressed as the God of Love, with bow and quiver, dancing around, and, with an early-ripened instinct, directing his arrow at the most beautiful and fascinating ladies in the room.

Prince Henry paid no attention to all this; his wandering glance sought only the beautiful Louise, and a deep sigh escaped him at not having found her. Hastily he stepped through the rows of dancers which separated the two cavaliers from him.

"It appears," murmured Baron Kalkreuth to his friend, "it appears to me that the prince would like to get rid of us. He wishes to be entirely unobserved. I think we can profit by this, and therefore I shall take leave of you for a while, and seek my own adventures."

"I advise you," murmured Baron Kaphengst, laughingly, "to appoint no rendezvous for to-morrow."

"And why not, friend?"

"Because you will not be able to appear; for you will doubtless be in arrest."

"That is true, and I thank you for your prudent advice, and shall arrange all my rendezvous for the day after to-morrow. Farewell."

Baron Kaphengst turned laughingly to another part of the saloon. Suddenly he felt a hand placed on his shoulder, and a low voice murmured his name.

Terrified, he turned. "I am not the one you seek, mask," he said; but as he met those two large, burning eyes, he shuddered, and even his bold, daring heart stood still a moment from terror. Only the king had such eyes; only he had such a commanding glance.

"You say you are not the one I seek," said the mask. "Well, yes, you speak wisely. I sought in you a brave and obedient officer, and it appears that you are not that. You are not, then, Lieutenant von Kaphengst?"

Kaphengst thought a moment. He was convinced it was the king that spoke with him, for Frederick had not attempted to disguise his voice. Kaphengst knew he was discovered. There remained nothing for him but to try and reconcile the king by a jest.

He bowed close to the king, and whispered: "Listen, mask—as you have recognized me, I will acknowledge the truth. Yes, I am Lieutenant von Kaphengst, and am incognito. You understand me—I came to this ball incognito. He is a scoundrel who repeats it!" and, without awaiting an answer, he hastened away to seek the prince and Baron Kalkreuth, acquaint them with the king's presence, and fly with them from his anger.

But Prince Henry, whose fruitless search for his sweetheart had made him angry and defiant, declared he would remain at the ball until it was over, and that it should be optional with the king to insult his brother openly, and to punish and humble a prince of his house before the world.

"I, unfortunately, do not belong to the princes of the royal house, and I therefore fear that the king might regard me as the cat who had to pull the hot chestnuts from the ashes, and I might suffer for all three. I therefore pray your highness to allow me to withdraw."

"You may go, and if you meet Kalkreuth, ask him to accompany you. You officers must not carry your insubordination any further. I, as prince, and Hohenzollern, dare the worst, but, be assured, I shall pay for my presumption. Farewell, and hasten! Do not forget Kalkreuth."

Kaphengst sought in vain. Kalkreuth was nowhere to be found, and he had to wend his way alone to Potsdam.

"I shall take care not to await the order of the king for my arrest," said Baron Kaphengst to himself, as he rode down the road to Potsdam. "I shall be in arrest when his order arrives. Perhaps that will soften his anger."

Accordingly, when Kaphengst arrived at the court guard, in Potsdam, he assumed the character of a drunken, quarrelsome officer, and played his role so well that the commander placed him in arrest.

An hour later the king's order reached the commander to arrest Baron Kaphengst, and with smiling astonishment he received the answer that he had been under arrest for the last hour.

In the mean time, Kaphengst had not miscalculated. The prince was put under arrest for eight days, Kalkreuth for three. He was released the next morning, early enough to appear at the parade. As the king, with his generals, rode down to the front, he immediately noticed the audacious young officer, whose eye met his askance and pleadingly. The king beckoned to him, and as Baron Kaphengst stood erect before him, the king said, laughingly; "It is truly difficult to exchange secrets with one of your height; bow down to me, I have something to whisper in you ear."

The comrades and officers, yes, even the generals, saw not without envy that the king was so gracious to the young Lieutenant von Kaphengst; whispered a few words to him confidentially, and then smiling and bowing graciously, moved on.

It was, therefore, natural that, when the king left, all were anxious to congratulate the young lieutenant, and ask him what the king had whispered. But Baron Kaphengst avoided, with dignified gravity, all inquiries, and only whispered to his commander softly, but loud enough for every one to hear, the words, "State secrets," then bowing profoundly, returned with an earnest and grave face to his dwelling, there to meditate at his leisure upon the king's words—words both gracious and cruel, announcing his advancement, but at the same time condemning him to secrecy.

The king's words were: "You are a captain, but he is a scoundrel who repeats it!"

Thus Baron Kaphengst was captain, but no one suspected it; the captain remained a simple lieutenant in the eyes of the world.

CHAPTER VI
THE LEGACY OF VON TRENCK, COLONEL OF THE PANDOURS

Baron Weingarten, the new secretary of legation of the Austrian embassy in Berlin, paced the ambassador's office in great displeasure. It was the hour in which all who had affairs to arrange with the Austrian ambassador, passports to vise, contracts to sign, were allowed entrance, and it was the baron's duty to receive them. But no one came; no one desired to make use of his ability or his mediation, and this displeased the baron and put him out of humor. It was not the want of work and activity that annoyed him; the baron would have welcomed the dolce far niente had it not been unfortunately connected with his earnings; the fees he received for passports, and the arrangement of other affairs, formed part of his salary as secretary of legation, and as he possessed no fortune, this was his only resource. This indigence alone led him to resign his aristocratic independence and freedom of action. He had not entered the state service from ambition, but for money, that he might have the means of supporting his mother and unmarried sisters, and enable himself to live according to his rank and old aristocratic name. Baron Weingarten would have made any sacrifice, submitted to any service, to obtain wealth. Poverty had demoralized him, pride had laid a mildew on his heart and stifled all noble aspirations. As he read a letter, just received from his mother, complaining of wants and privations, telling of the attachment of a young officer to his sister, and that poverty alone prevented their marriage, his heart was filled with repining, and at this moment he was prepared to commit a crime, if, by so doing, he could have obtained wealth.

In this despairing and sorrowful mood he had entered the office, and awaited in vain for petitioners who would pay him richly for his services. But the hours passed in undisturbed quiet, and Baron Weingarten was in the act of leaving the office, as the servant announced Baron von Waltz, and the court councillor, Zetto, from Vienna.

He advanced to meet the two gentlemen, with a smiling countenance, and welcomed his Austrian countrymen heartily.

The two gentlemen seated themselves silently; Weingarten took a seat in front of them.

A painful, embarrassed pause ensued. The majestic Baron von Waltz looked silently at the ceiling, while the black, piercing eyes of the little Councillor Zetto examined the countenance of Weingarten with a strangely searching and penetrating expression.

"You are from Vienna?" said Weingarten at last, putting an end to this painful silence.

"We are from Vienna," answered the baron, with a grave bow. "And have travelled here post-haste to have an interview with you."

"With me?" asked the secretary of legation, astonished.

"With you alone," said the baron, gravely.

"We wish you to do the King of Prussia a great service," said Zetto, solemnly.

Weingarten reddened, and said confusedly: "The King of Prussia! You forget, gentlemen, that my services belong alone to the Empress Maria Theresa."

"He defends himself before he is accused," said Zetto, aside. "It is then true, as we have been told, he is playing a double game—serves Austria and Prussia at the same time." Turning to Baron Weingarten, he said: "That which we ask of you will be at the same time a service to our gracious empress, for certainly it would not only distress, but compromise her majesty, if an Austrian officer committed a murder in Prussia."

"Murder!" cried the secretary of legation.

"Yes, an intentional murder," said Baron Waltz, emphatically—"the murder of the King of Prussia. If you prevent this crime, you will receive ten thousand guilders," said Zetto, examining Weingarten's countenance closely. He remarked that the baron, who was but a moment ago pale from terror, now reddened, and that his eyes sparkled joyously.

"And what can I do to prevent this murder?" asked Weingarten, hastily.

"You can warn the king."

"But to warn successfully, I must have proofs."

"We are ready to give the most incontrovertible proofs."

"I must, before acting, be convinced of the veracity of your charges."

"I hope that my word of honor will convince you of their truth," said Baron Waltz, pathetically.

Weingarten bowed, with an ambiguous smile, that did not escape Zetto. He drew forth his pocket-book, and took from it a small, folded paper, which he handed to Weingarten.

"If I strengthen my declaration with this paper, will you trust me?"

Weingarten looked with joyful astonishment at the paper; it was a check for two thousand guilders. "My sister's dowry," thought Weingarten, with joy. But the next moment came doubt and suspicion. What if they were only trying him—only convincing themselves if he could be bought? Perhaps he was suspected of supplying the Prussian Government from time to time with Austrian news—of communicating to them the contents of important dispatches!

The fire faded from his eye, and with a firm countenance he laid the paper upon the table.

"Your are mistaken, gentlemen! That is no document, but a check."

"With which many documents could be purchased," said Zetto, smiling. Placing the paper again in his pocket-book, he took out another and a larger one. It was a check for three thousand guilders.

But Weingarten had regained his composure. He knew that men acting thus must be spies or criminals; that they were testing him, or luring him on to some unworthy act. In either case, he must be on his guard.

"I beg you to confirm your charge in the usual manner," said he, with a cold, indifferent glance at the paper. "Murder is a dreadful accusation—you cannot act too carefully. You say that an Austrian officer intends to murder the King of Prussia. How do you know this?"

"From himself," said Baron Waltz. "He communicated his intentions to me, and confided to me his entire plan."

"It appears," remarked Weingarten, mockingly, "that the officer had reason to believe he might trust you with this terrible secret."

"You see, however, that he was mistaken," said the baron, smilingly. "I demand of you to warn the King of Prussia of the danger that threatens him."

"I shall be compelled to make this danger clear, give all particulars, or the king will laugh at my story and consider it a fairy tale."

"You shall give him convincing proof. Say to him that the murder is to be committed when his majesty attends the Austrian review at Königsberg."

"How will the officer cross the Prussian border?"

"He is supplied with an Austrian passport, and under the pretence of inheriting a large property in Prussia, he has obtained leave of absence for a month."

"There remains now but one question: why does the officer wish to murder the king? What motive leads him to do so?"

"Revenge," said Baron von Waltz, solemnly—"an act of vengeance. This Austrian officer who is resolved to murder the king of Prussia, is Frederick von Trenck."

Weingarten was embarrassed, and his countenance bore an uneasy and troubled expression. But as his eye fell upon the weighty paper that lay before him, he smiled, and looked resolved.

"Now I have but one thing more to ask. Why, if your story is authentic, and well calculated to startle even the brave king, have you thought it necessary to remove my doubts with this document?"

Baron Waltz was silent, and looked inquiringly at Zetto.

"Why did I hand you this document?" said the councillor, with a sweet smile. "Because gold remains gold, whether received from an Austrian councillor or from a Prussian prince."

"Sir, do you dare to insult me?" cried the secretary of legation, fiercely.

Zetto smiled. "No, I only wish to notify you that we are aware that it is through you that Baron von Trenck receives money from a certain aristocratic lady in Berlin. It is, therefore, most important that the king should be warned by you of his intended murder—otherwise you might be thought an accomplice."

Weingarten appeared not to be in the least disconcerted by this statement—he seemed not even to have heard it.

"Before I warn the king," he said, with calm composure, "I must be convinced of the truth of the story myself, and I acknowledge to you that I am not convinced, cannot understand your motives for seeking the destruction of Baron von Trenck."

"Ah! you search into our motives—you mistrust us," cried Zetto, hastily. "Well, we will prove to you that we trust you, by telling you our secret. You know the story of the inheritance of Trenck?"

"He is the only heir of the pandour chieftain, Franz von Trenck."

"Correct. And do you know the history of this pandour chieftain Trenck?"

"I have heard a confused and uncertain statement, but nothing definite or reliable."

"It is, however, a very interesting and instructive story, and shows how far a man with a determined will and great energy can reach, when his thoughts are directed to one end. Baron Trenck wished to be rich, immensely rich—that was the aim of his life. Seduced by his love of money, he became the captain of a band of robbers, then a murderer, a church-robber; from that a brave soldier, and, at last, a holy penitent. Robbing and plundering everywhere, he succeeded in collecting millions. The pandour chieftain Trenck soon became so rich, that he excited the envy of the noblest and wealthiest men in the kingdom, so rich that he was able to lend large sums of money to the powerful and influential Baron Lowenwalde. You see, baron, it only needs a determined will to become rich."

"Oh! the foolish man," said Weingarten, shrugging his shoulders. "Lending money to a noble and powerful man, is making an irreconcilable enemy."

"You speak like a prophet. It happened, as you say. Lowenwalde became Trenck's enemy. He accused him of embezzling the imperial money, of treachery and faithlessness—and Trenck was imprisoned."

"His millions obtained his release, did they not?"

"No. His riches reduced him to greater misery. His lands were sequestered, and a body of commissioners were selected to attend to them. Baron Waltz and myself belonged to this commission."

"Ah! I begin to understand," murmured Weingarten.

Baron Zetto continued, with a smile. "The commissioners made the discovery that report had greatly exaggerated the riches of Trenck. He had not many treasures, but many debts. In order to liquidate those debts, we desired his creditors to announce themselves every day, and promised them a daily ducat until the end of the process."

"I hope you two gentlemen were among his creditors," said Weingarten.

"Certainly, we were, and also Baron Marken."

"Therefore you have a threefold advantage from Trenck's imprisonment. First, your salary as a member of the commission; secondly, as a creditor—"

"And thirdly—you spoke of a threefold advantage?"

"And thirdly," said Weingarten, laughing, "in searching for the missing treasures of Baron Trenck which had disappeared so unfortunately."

"Ah, sir, you speak like those who suspected us at court, and wished to make the empress believe that we had enriched ourselves as commissioners. Soon after this Trenck died, and Frederick von Trenck hastened from St. Petersburg to receive his inheritance. How great was his astonishment to find instead of the hoped-for millions a few mortgaged lands, an income of a hundred thousand guilders, and sixty-three creditors who claimed the property."

"He should have become one of the commissioners," remarked Weingarten, mockingly. "Perhaps it would have then been easier for him to obtain his possessions."

"He attempted it in another way, with the aid of money, bribery, and persuasion. He has already succeeded in obtaining fifty-four of his sixty-three processes, and will win the others in a few days."

"And then he will doubtless cause the commissioners to give in their accounts, and close their books."

"Exactly. He has already commenced to do so. He ordered an investigation to be made against the quartermaster, and the commander of the regiment to which Franz von Trenck belonged. This man had accused Trenck of having embezzled eight thousand of the imperial money, and Trenck succeeded so far, that it was declared that it was not he, but his accusers, who had committed the crime. The consequence was, that the quartermaster was deposed, and it would have fared as badly with the commander, had he not found powerful protection."

"And now the dangerous Frederick von Trenck will seize the property of the commissioners."

"He would do so if we did not know how to prevent him. We must employ every means to remove him, and, believe me, we are not the only men who wish for his disappearance. A large and powerful party have the same desire, and will joyfully pay ten thousand guilders to be freed from his investigations."

Weingarten's eyes sparkled for a moment, and his heart beat quickly, but he suppressed these joyful emotions, and retained his calm and indifferent expression.

"Gentlemen," he said, quietly, "as you are speaking of a real criminal, one who intends committing so great a crime, I am at your service, and no money or promises are necessary to buy my assistance."

"Is he really a man of honor, and have we received false information?" thought Zetto, who was misled for a moment by the quiet and virtuous looks of the secretary of legation.

"In the mean while you will not prevent those for whom you are about to do a great service from showing their gratitude," said Baron Waltz. "Every one has a right to give or to receive a present."

"Gentlemen," said Baron Weingarten, smilingly, "No one has spoken of a present, but of a payment, a bribery, and you can readily understand that this is insulting to a man of honor."

"Ah, he leaves open a door of escape," thought Zetto. "He is won, he can be bought.—You are right, baron," he said aloud, "and we are wrong to offer you now that which hereafter will be a debt of gratitude. We will speak no more of this, but of the danger that threatens the king. You alone can save him by warning him of his danger."

"You really believe, then, that Trenck has the intention of murdering the king?" said Weingarten.

"We will believe it," said Zetto, with an ambiguous smile.

"We must believe it!" cried Baron Waltz, emphatically. "We must either believe in his murderous intentions, or be ourselves regarded as traitors and robbers. You will think it natural that we prefer the first alternative, and as he resolved to ruin us, we will anticipate him, and set the trap into which he must fall."

"Why could you not lay your snares in Austria, gentlemen? Why could you not accuse him of intending to murder the empress?"

Zetto shrugged his shoulders. "That would not be credible, because Trenck has no motive for murdering Maria Theresa, while he might very well thirst to revenge himself upon Frederick. You know that the king and Trenck are personal enemies. Trenck has boasted of this enmity often and loud enough to be understood by the whole world, and I do not believe that this animosity has diminished. Enemies naturally desire to destroy each other. Trenck would succeed if we did not warn the king, and enable him to anticipate his enemy."

"How can this be done? Will the king really go to Konigsberg to be present at the Austrian festivities?"

"It has been spoken of."

"Well, Trenck now proposes to go to Dantzic, and he has boasted that he will enter Konigsberg at the same time with the King of Prussia, who will not dare to arrest him."

"We have made a bet with him of a hundred louis d'or on this boast," said Baron Waltz, "and for greater security we have put it in writing."

"Have you it with you?"

"Here it is."

The baron handed Weingarten a paper, which he seized hastily, unfolded, and read several times.

"This is indeed written in very ambiguous language, and calculated to ruin Trenck should it reach the hands of the king," said Baron Weingarten with a cruel smile.

Zetto returned this smile. "I wrote the document, and you will naturally understand that I measured the words very closely."

"Who copied the letter?" asked Weingarten. "Doubtlessly Baron Trenck was not magnanimous enough to do that."

"Baron Waltz is a great adept in imitating handwriting, and he happily possessed original letters of Trenck's," said Zetto, smilingly.

"You will find it most natural that I should try to win my bet," said Baron Waltz. "If Trenck is arrested before he goes to Konigsberg, I have won my bet, and will receive the hundred louis d'ors from the commissioners."

All three laughed.

"These commissioners will soon have to pay you ten thousand guilders," whispered Zetto. "Here is a bond. On the day that Trenck is a prisoner of the king of Prussia, this bond is due, and you will then find that the commissioners are not backward in paying." Zetto laid the document upon the table. "You will now have the kindness to receive our testimony, and, if you desire it, we will add our accusations, or you can mention that this can be done."

Weingarten did not answer; a repentant fear tormented his heart, and for a moment it appeared as if his good and evil genius were struggling for his soul.

"This involves probably the life of a man," he said, softly; "it is a terrible accusation that I must pronounce: if not condemned to death, the king will imprison him for many long years, and I shall be responsible for this injustice."

Councillor Zetto's attentive ear heard every word; he stood near him like the evil one, and his piercing eyes rested upon the agitated countenance of Weingarten and read his thoughts.

"Have you not lived the life of a prisoner for many years?" asked Zetto, in a low, unnatural voice; "have you not always been a slave of poverty? Will you now, from weak pity, lose the opportunity of freeing yourself from this bondage? Ten thousand guilders is no fortune, but it may be the beginning of one—it may be the thread of Ariadne to lead you from the labyrinth of poverty to freedom and light; and who will thank you if you do not seize this thread—who recompense you for your generosity and magnanimity? If you tell it to the wise and cunning, they will laugh at you, and if the foolish hear it, they will not understand you. Every one is the moulder of his own happiness, and woe unto him who neglects to forge the iron while it is hot!"

Baron Weingarten felt each of these words. He did not know if they were uttered by human lips, or if they came from the depths of his own base soul.

"It is true, it is true!" he cried, in a frightened voice, "He is a fool who does not seize the hand of Fortune when tendered by the laughing goddess—a fool who does not break his fetters when he has the power to rend them. Come, gentlemen! We take the testimony, and when that is done, I will conduct you to our ambassador, Baron Puebla."

"Not so—when that is done, we shall depart with post-haste; you alone shall receive thanks and recompense. Now to work!"

CHAPTER VII
THE KING AND WEINGARTEN

The king paced his room hastily; he was very pale, his lip trembled, and his eyes sparkled angrily.

He suddenly remained standing before the Austrian secretary of legation, and gazed long and earnestly into his face, but his glance, before which so many had trembled, was sustained by the secretary with so quiet and innocent a countenance that it deceived even the king.

"I see that you are convinced of the truth of what you tell me." the king said at last. "You really believe that this madman has the intention of murdering me?"

"I am convinced of it, sire," replied Weingarten, humbly, "for I have the proof of his intention in my hand."

"The proof—what proof?"

"This paper which I allowed myself to hand to your majesty, and which you laid upon the table without reading."

"Ah, it is true! I forgot that in my excitement," said the king, mildly. "I beg you to read me the contents of this paper."

Baron Weingarten received the paper from the king with a respectful bow; his voice did not tremble in the least as he read the important words which refined malice and cruel avarice had written there—words which, if literally interpreted, would fully condemn Trenck.

The words were:

"'In consequence of a bet, I pledge myself to be in Konigsberg the same day in which the King Frederick of Prussia, my cruel enemy and persecutor, shall arrive there. I shall go there to do, in the king's presence, that which no one has done before me, and which no one will do after me. If I do not succeed in accomplishing my purpose, or if I should be arrested, I have lost my bet, and shall owe Baron Waltz one hundred louis d'or, which must be paid him by the commissioners of the Trenck estate.'"

"'BARON FREDERICK VON TRENCK.'"

"And Trenck wrote this note himself?" said the king.

"If your majesty is acquainted with Trenck's handwriting, you will perhaps have the goodness to examine it yourself."

"I know his handwriting; give me the paper."

He took the paper and glanced over it searchingly. "It is his handwriting," he murmured; "but I will examine it again."

Speaking thus, he stepped hastily to his escritoire, and took from a small box several closely written yellow papers, and compared them with the document which Weingarten had given him.

Ah, how little did Trenck dream, as he wrote those letters, that they would witness against him, and stamp him as a criminal! They were already a crime in the king's eyes, for they were tender letters that Trenck had dared to write from Vienna to the Princess Amelia. They had never reached her!

And not those tender epistles of a tearful and unhappy love must bear witness against the writer, and condemn him for the second time!

"It is his handwriting," said the king, as he laid the letters again in the box. "I thank you, Baron Weingarten, you have saved me from a disagreeable occurrence, for, if I will not even believe that Trenck intended murder, he was at all events willing to create a scene, if only to gratify his vanity. It appears that he has now played out his role at Vienna, as well as in St. Petersburg and Berlin, and the world would forget him if he did not attract its attention by some mad piece of folly. How he intended to accomplish this I do not know, but certainly not by a murder—no, I cannot believe that!"

"Your majesty is always noble and magnanimous, but it appears to me that these words can have but one meaning. 'I shall go to Konigsberg,' writes Baron Trenck, 'and there do in the presence of the king what no one has done before me, and what no one will do after me.' Does not this make his intention pretty clear?"

"Only for those who know his intentions or suspect them, for others they could have any other signification, some romantic threat, nothing more. Baron Trenck is a known adventurer, a species of Don Quixote, always fighting against windmills, and believing that warriors and kings honor him so far as to be his enemies. I punished Trenck when he was in my service, for insubordination; now he is no longer in my service, and I have forgotten him, but woe be unto him if he forces me to remember him!"

"Your majesty will soon see if he is falsely accused. These reliable and irreproachable men came especially to warn your majesty, through me. You will discover if they have calumniated Trenck, by giving this testimony. If he does not go to Dantzic, does not enter Prussia, they have sworn falsely, and Trenck is innocent."

"He will not dare to cross the borders of my state, for he knows he will be court-martialled as a deserter. But I am convinced that he is a bold adventurer, he has boasted that he will defy me, that is certainly what no one has done before him, and what no one will do after him, but it will rest there, you may believe me."

Baron Weingarten bowed silently. The king continued, with an engaging smile.

"However, monsieur, I owe you many thanks, and it would please me to have an opportunity of rewarding you."

Until this moment, Weingarten had been standing with bowed head, he now stood erect, and his eye dared to meet that of the king.

"Sire," he said, with the noble expression of offended innocence, "I demand and wish no other reward than that you may profit by my warning. If the fearful danger that threatens your majesty is averted through me, that will be my all-sufficient recompense. I must decline any other."

The king smiled approvingly. "You speak emphatically, and it appears that you really believe in this danger. Well, I thank you only as that is your desire. I will respect your warning and guard myself from the danger that you believe threatens me, but to do that, and at the same time to convince ourselves of Trenck's evil intentions, we must observe the most perfect silence in this whole affair, and you must promise me to speak of it to no one."

"Sire, secrecy appeared to me so necessary, that I did not even communicate it to Baron Puebla, but came to your majesty on my own responsibility."

"You did well, for now Trenck will fall unwarned into the trap we set for him. Be silent, therefore, upon the subject. If you should ever have a favor to ask, come to me with this tabatiere in your hand. I will remember this hour, and if it is in my power will grant you what you wish."

He handed Weingarten his gold, diamond-studded tabatiere, and received his thanks with approving smiles. After he had dismissed the secretary of legation, and was alone, the smile faded from his face, and his countenance was sad and disturbed.

"It has come to this," he said, as he paced his room, with his hands folded behind his back. "This man, whom I once loved so warmly, wishes to murder me. Ah! ye proud princes, who imagine yourselves gods on earth, you are not even safe from a murderer's dagger, and you are as vulnerable as the commonest beggar. Why does he wish my death? Were I a fantastic, romantic hero, I might say he hoped to claim his sweetheart over my dead body! But Amelia is no longer a person for whom a man would risk his life; she is but a faint and sad resemblance of the past—her rare beauty is tear-stained and turned to ashes, but her heart still lives; it is young and warm, and belongs to Trenck! And shall I dissipate this last illusion? Must she now learn that he to whom she sacrificed so much is but a common murderer? No, I will spare her this sorrow! I will not give Trenck the opportunity to fulfil his work; even his intention shall remain doubtful. I shall not go to Konigsberg; and if, in his presumptuous thirst for notoriety or for vengeance, he should enter Prussia, he shall be cared for—he shall not escape his punishment. Let him but try to cross my borders—he will find a snare spread, a cage from which he cannot escape. Yes, so it shall be. But neither the world nor Trenck shall suspect why this is done. If my brothers and envious persons hold him up in future as an example of my hardness of heart, what do I care for their approval, or the praise of short-sighted men! I do my duty, and am answerable only to God and myself. Trenck intends to murder me—I must preserve myself for my people. My mission is not yet accomplished; and if a poisonous insect crosses my path, I must crush it."

CHAPTER VIII
THE UNWILLING BRIDEGROOM

Prince Henry had again passed eight days in arrest—eight tedious days, days of powerless anger and painful humiliation. This arrest had been, by the king's express orders, so strict, that no one was allowed to see the prince but Pollnitz, who belonged, as the king said, to the inventory of the house of Hohenzollern, and, therefore, all doors were open to him.

Pollnitz alone had, therefore, the pleasure of hearing the complaints, and reproaches, and bitter accusations of the prince against his brother. Pollnitz always had an attentive ear for these complaints; and after listening to the prince with every appearance of real feeling and warm sympathy, he would hasten to the king, and with drooping eyelids and rejoicing heart repeat the bitter and hateful words of the unsuspicious prince—words that were well calculated to increase the king's displeasure. The prince still declared that he would not marry, and the king insisted that he must submit to his will and commands.

Thus the eight days had passed, and Pollnitz came to-day with the joyful news that his arrest was at an end, and he was now free.

"That means," said the prince, bitterly, "that I am free to wander through the stupid streets of Potsdam; appear at his table; that my clothes may be soiled by his unbearable four-legged friends, and my ears deafened by the dull, pedantic conversation of his no less unbearable two-legged friends."

"Your highness can save yourself from all these small annoyances," said Pollnitz; "you have only to marry."

"Marry, bah! That means to give my poor sister-in-law, Elizabeth Christine, a companion, that they may sing their sorrows to each other. No, I have not the bravery of my kingly brother, to make a feeling, human being unhappy in order to satisfy state politics. No, I possess not the egotism to purchase my freedom with the life-long misery of another."

"But, mon Dieu! my prince," said Pollnitz, in his cynical way, "you look at it in too virtuous a manner. All women are not as good and pure as poor Elizabeth Christine, and know how to compensate themselves in other quarters for the indifference of their husbands. We are not speaking here of a common marriage, but of the betrothal of a prince. You do not marry your heart, but your hand. Truly such a marriage-ceremony is a protecting talisman, that may be held up to other women as an iron shield upon which, all their egotistical wishes, all their extravagant demands must rebound. Moreover, a married man is entirely sans consequence for all unmarried women, and if they should love such a one, the happy mortal may be convinced that his love is really a caprice of the heart, and not a selfish calculation or desire to marry."

The prince regarded the smiling courtier earnestly, almost angrily. "Do you know," he said, "that what you say appears to me very immoral?"

"Immoral?" asked Pollnitz, astonished; "what is that? Your princely highness knows that I received my education at the French court, under the protection of the Regent of Orleans and the Princess of the Palatinate, and there I never heard this word immoral. Perhaps your highness will have the kindness to explain it to me."

"That would be preaching to deaf ears," said the prince, shrugging his shoulders. "We will not quarrel about the meaning of a word. I only wish to make you understand that I would not marry at my brother's bon plaisir. I will not continue this race of miserable princes, that are entirely useless, and consequently a burden to the state. Oh! if Heaven would only give me the opportunity to distinguish myself before this people, and give to this name that is go small, so unworthy, a splendor, a color, a signification!"

"Your highness is ambitous," said Pollnitz, as the prince, now silent, paced his room with deep emotion.

"Yes, I am ambitious—I thirst for action, renown, and activity. I despise this monotonous, colorless existence, without end or aim. By God! how happy I should be, if, instead of a prince, I could be a simple private man, proprietor of a small landed estate, with a few hundred subjects, that I should endeavor to make happy! But I am nothing but a king's brother, have nothing but my empty title and the star upon my coat. My income is so small, so pitiful, that it would scarcely suffice to pay the few servants I have, if, at the same time, they were not paid by the king as his spies."

"But all this will cease as soon as you speak the decisive word; as soon as you declare yourself prepared to marry."

"And you dare to tell me this?" cried the prince, with flashing eyes— "you, that know I love a lady who is unfortunately no princess; or do you believe that a miserable prince has not the heart of a man—that he does not possess the ardent desire, the painful longing for the woman he loves?"

"Oh, women do not deserve that we should love them so ardently; they are all fickle and inconstant, believe me, my prince."

The prince cast a quick, questioning glance at the smiling countenance of the courtier.

"Why do you say this to me?" he asked, anxiously.

"Because I am convinced of its truth, your highness; because I believe no woman has the power to preserve her love when obstacles are placed in the way, or that she can be faithful for the short space of eight days, if her lover is absent."

The prince was startled, and looked terrified at Pollnitz.

"Eight days," he murmured; "it is eight days—no, it is twelve since I saw Louise."

"Ah, twelve days—and your highness has the really heroic belief that she still loves you?"

The prince sighed, and his brow clouded, but only for a few moments, and his countenance was again bright and his eyes sparkled.

"Yes, I have this belief; and why should I not have it, as my own heart had stood the trial? I have not seen her for twelve days, have not heard of her, and still my love is as great and as ardent as ever. Yes, I believe that at the thought of her my heart beats more quickly, more longingly than if I had her in my arms."

"The reason of this," said Pollnitz, almost sympathetically, "is that it is your first love."

Prince Henry looked at him angrily.

"You are wrong and most unjust to this beautiful woman, who remained good and pure in the midst of the corrupting and terrible circumstances in which destiny placed her. She preserved a chaste heart, an unspotted soul. Her misfortunes only refined her, and therefore I love her, and believe that God has placed me in her way that, after all her sufferings, I might make her happy. Oh, precisely because of her sorrows, the shameful slanders with which she is pursued, and all for which she is reproached, I love her."

"Well, my prince," sighed Pollnitz, with a tragical expression, "I never saw a bolder hero and a more pious Christian than your highness."

"What do you mean by that, Pollnitz?"

"That an enormous amount of bravery is necessary, prince, to believe Madame von Kleist chaste and innocent, and that only a pious Christian can count himself so entirely among those of whom Christ says, 'Blessed are they that have not seen and yet have believed.' May a good fairy long preserve you your bravery and your Christianity! But surely your highness must have important and convincing proofs to believe in the innocence and faithfulness of this woman. I confess that any other man would have been discouraged in his godlike belief by facts. It is a fact that for twelve days Madame von Kleist has sent you no message through me; it is a fact that she was not at the masked ball; that as often as I have been to her in these last days, to deliver letters for your highness, and to obtain hers in return, she has never received me, always excused herself; and, therefore, I could not receive her letters, nor deliver those of your highness."

"And were you not in Berlin early this morning! Did you not go to her as I ordered you, and tell her she might expect me this evening?"

"I went to her house, but in vain; she was with the queen-mother, and I was told that she would not return until late in the evening, I therefore could not deliver the message, your highness."

The prince stamped his foot impatiently, and walked hastily to and fro; his brow was clouded, his lips trembled with inward emotion. The sharp eye of the baron followed with an attentive, pitiless glance every movement of his face, noted every sigh that came from his anxious heart, that he might judge whether the seeds of mistrust that he had sown in the breast of the prince would grow. But Prince Henry was still young, brave, and hopeful; it was his first love they wished to poison, but his young, healthy nature withstood the venom, and vanquished its evil effects. His countenance resumed its quiet, earnest expression, and the cloud disappeared from his brow.

"Do you know," he said, standing before Pollnitz, and looking smilingly into his cunning face—"do you know that you do not descend, as the rest of mankind, from Adam and Eve, but in a direct line from the celebrated serpent? And truly you do honor to your ancestor! No paradise is holy to you, and to do evil gives you pleasure. But you shall not disturb my paradise; and as much of the old Adam as is still in me, I will not be foolish enough to eat of the bitter fruit that you offer me. No, you shall not succeed in making me jealous and distrustful; you shall not destroy my faith: and see you, those that believe are still in paradise, notwithstanding your ancestor, the serpent."

"My prince," said Pollnitz, shrugging his shoulders, "your highness looks upon me as a kind of Messiah—at least it pleases you to give me a mother and no father. But oh, my prince! if you are right about my descent, philosophers are certainly wrong, for they maintain that the serpent of paradise left gold as a fearful inheritance to mankind. I shall accuse my great-grandmother the serpent of disinheriting me and condemning me to live upon the generosity of my friends and patrons."

He looked at the prince, with a sly, covetous glance, but he had not understood him; engaged in deep thought, he had stepped to the window, and was gazing up at the heavens, where the clouds were chasing each other.

"She will be the entire day with my mother, and I shall not see her," he murmured. Then, turning hastily to Pollnitz, he asked, "How is the queen-mother? Did I not hear that she was suffering?"

"Certainly, your highness, a severe attack of gout confines her to her chair, and holds her prisoner."

"Poor mother! it is long since I saw you."

"It is true, the queen complained of it the last time I spoke with her," said Pollnitz, with a perfectly serious face, but with inward rejoicing.

Another pause ensued. The prince appeared to reflect, and to struggle with his own thoughts and wishes. Pollnitz stood behind him, and noted every motion, every sigh that he uttered, with his malicious smiles.

"I believe," said the prince, with still averted face, perhaps to prevent Pollnitz from seeing his blushes—"I believe it would be proper for me to inquire to-day personally after my mother's health; it is not only my duty to do so, but the desire of my heart."

"Her majesty will be pleased to see her beloved son again, and this pleasure will hasten her recovery."

The prince turned hastily and glanced sharply at Pollnitz, as if he wished to read his inmost thoughts. But the countenance of the courtier was earnest and respectful.

"If that is your opinion," said the prince, with a happy smile, "my duty as a son demands that I should hasten to the queen, and I will go immediately to Berlin. But as I am going to my mother, and solely on her account, I will do it in the proper form. Have, therefore, the kindness to obtain my leave of the king—bring me my brother's answer immediately, I only await it to depart."

"And I hasten to bring it to your highness," said Pollnitz, withdrawing.

Prince Henry looked thoughtfully after him.

"I shall see her," he murmured; "I shall speak with her, and shall learn why she withdrew herself so long from me. Oh, I know she will be able to justify herself, and these slanders and evil reports will flee before her glance as clouds before the rays of the sun."

In the mean while, Pollnitz hastened to Sans Souci, where he was immediately received by the king.

"Your majesty," he said, joyfully, "the young lion has fallen into the net that we set for him."

"He goes then to Berlin, to the queen-mother?" asked the king, quickly.

"He begs your majesty's permission to take this little trip."

"He really charged you with this commission?"

"Yes, sire: it appears that his obstinacy is beginning to relent, and that he thinks of submitting."

The king was silent, and walked thoughtfully to and fro, with clouded brow, then remained standing before Pollnitz, and looked sharply and piercingly at him.

"You rejoice," he said, coldly, "but you only think of your own advantage. You are indifferent to the sorrow we are preparing for my brother. You only think that your debts will be paid. Yes, I will pay them, but I shall never forget that you have betrayed my brother's confidence."

"I only acted according to your majesty's commands," said Pollnitz, confounded. "Certainly, but if you had resisted my commands, I would have esteemed and prized you the more. Now, I shall pay your debts, but I shall despise you. No one has reasons for thanking you."

"Sire, I desire no other thanks. Had I been paid with money for my services, instead of fine speeches, I would have been as rich as Croesus."

"And a beggar in virtue," said the king, smiling. "But go, I was wrong to reproach you. I shall now go to Berlin, and when my brother arrives he shall find me there. Go now, my grand chamberlain, and take the prince my permission for a three days' absence."

CHAPTER IX
THE FIRST DISAPPOINTMENT

A few hours later the equipage of Prince Henry arrived in the court-yard of Monbijou, and the prince demanded of his mother, the widowed queen, permission to pay her his respects.

Sophia Dorothea was suffering greatly. The gout, that slow but fatal disease, which does not kill at once, but limb by limb, had already paralyzed the feet of the poor queen, and confined her to her chair. To-day her sufferings were greater than usual, and she was not able to leave her bed. Therefore, she could not receive the prince as a queen, but only as a mother, without ceremony or etiquette. That the meeting might be entirely without constraint, the maids of honor left the queen's room, and as the prince entered, he saw the ladies disappearing by another door; the last one had just made her farewell bow, and was kissing respectfully the queen's hand.

This was Louise von Kleist, for whose sake the prince had come, and for whom his heart throbbed painfully. He could have cried aloud for joy as he saw her in her bewildering loveliness, her luxuriant beauty. He longed to seize her hands and cover them with kisses—to tell her how much he had suffered, how much he was still suffering for her sake.

But Louise appeared not to have seen him, not to have noticed his entrance. She had only eyes and ears for the queen, who was just dismissing her with winning words, telling her to remain in the castle and return when she desired to see her.

"I shall remain and await your majesty's commands," said Louise, withdrawing hastily.

The queen now greeted the prince as if she had just observed him, and invited him to be seated on the fauteuil near her couch. The prince obeyed, but he was absent-minded and restless, and the more the queen endeavored to engage him in harmless and unconstrained conversation, the more monosyllabic and preoccupied he became. The poor prince remembered only that his beloved was so near, that only a door separated them, and prevented him from gazing on her beauty.

Yes, Louise was really in the next room, in the cabinet of the queen, sorrowful and exhausted; she had fallen upon the little sofa near the door, the smile had left her lips, and her brilliant, bewitching eyes were filled with tears. Louise wept; she wept for her last youthful dream, her last hope of happiness and virtue, for her sad, shadowed future and wounded pride; for to-day she had to resign forever the proud hopes, the brilliant future for which she had striven with so much energy.

But it was vain to struggle against this hard necessity. The king had given her his orders and was there to see them carried out. He sat behind that portiere that led into the grand saloon; he had just left Louise, and, before going, had said to her, in a stern, commanding tone:

"You will fulfil my commands accurately. You know that Fritz Wendel still lives, and that I shall be inexorable if you do not act as you have promised."

Louise submitted respectfully to the king's commands; she accepted her fate, but she wept bitterly, and when she felt that the king's eyes were no longer upon her, her tears flowed unceasingly. Perhaps Frederick still saw her, or suspected her weakness, for the portiere opened slightly, and his noble, but stern countenance appeared.

"Madame," he said, "if the prince sees you with tearful eyes, he will not believe in your happiness."

Louise smiled painfully. "Ah! sire, he will believe I am weeping for joy. I have often heard of joyful tears."

The king did not reply; he felt for her agony, and closed the partiere.

"I will cry no more," she said; "I have accepted my destiny, and will fulfil it bravely for the sake of my daughter. It concerns Camilla's happiness more than my own. I will deserve the respect of my unfortunate child."

In saying this, a smile like a sunbeam illuminated her countenance. But now she started up, and laid her hand in terror upon her heart. She heard steps approaching. The door moved, and in a moment the king appeared and motioned to her.

"Courage, courage!" murmured Louise, and with instinctive fear she flew away from the door and placed herself in the niche of the last window.

To reach her, the prince must cross the saloon; that would give her a few moments to recover. The door opened and Prince Henry entered; his glance flew quickly over the saloon, and found the one he sought.

Louise could have shrieked with agony when she saw the tender smile with which he greeted her. Never had he appeared so handsome, so noble as at this moment, when she must resign him forever.

But there was no time to think of this, no time for complaints or regrets. He was there, he stood before her, offered both his hands, and greeted her with the tenderest words of love.

Louise had a stern part to play, and she dared not listen to her heart's pleadings.

"Ah, my prince," she said, with a laugh that sounded to herself like the wail of a lost soul—"ah, my prince, take care! we women are very credulous, and I might take your jesting words for truth."

"I advise you to do so," said the prince, happy and unconcerned. "Yes, Louise, I advise you to do so, for you know well that my jesting words have an earnest meaning. And now that we are alone, we will dispense with ceremony. You must justify yourself before a lover—a lover who is unfortunately very jealous. Yes, yes, Louise, that is my weakness; I do not deny it, I am jealous—jealous of all those who keep you from me, who prevent my receiving your letters."

"My letters!" said Louise, astonished; "why should I have written letters to your highness? I do not believe it is the custom for ladies to write to gentlemen voluntarily. It has been two weeks since I received a letter from your highness."

"Because it was impossible for my messenger to deliver them, Louise: you were so unapproachable, at least for me. But you must have known that my thoughts were always with you, that my heart pined for news and comfort from you."

"Non, vraiment, I did not know it," said Louise, laughingly.

"You did not know it?" asked Henry, wonderingly. "Well, what did you suppose?"

"I thought," she said, carelessly—"I thought that Prince Henry had overcome or forgotten his little folly of the carnival."

"And then?"

"Then I determined to follow his example. Then I preached a long sermon to my foolish eyes—they were misty with tears. Listen, I said to them: 'You foolish things you have no reason to weep; you should always look bright and dazzling, even if you never see Prince Henry again. Really, the absence of the prince has been most fortunate for you. You might have whispered all kinds of foolish things to my weak heart. The prince is young, handsome, and amiable, and it amuses him to win the love of fair ladies. Had you seen him more frequently, it is possible he might have succeeded with poor Louise, and the little flirtation we carried on together would have resulted in earnest love on my part. That would have been a great misfortune. Laugh and look joyous, beautiful eyes, you have saved me from an unrequited love. You should not weep, but rejoice. Look around and find another suitor, who would, perhaps, love me so fondly that he could not forget me in a few days; whose love I might return with ardor.' This, my prince, is the sermon I preached to my eyes when they grew dim with tears."

"And was your sermon effective?" said the prince, with pale, trembling lips. "Did your eyes, those obedient slaves, look around and find another lover?"

"Ah! your highness, how can you doubt it? My eyes are indeed my slaves, and must obey. Yes, they looked and found the happiness they sought."

"What happiness," asked Henry, apparently quite tranquil, but he pressed his hand nervously on the chair that stood by him—"what happiness did your eyes find?"

Louise looked at him and sighed deeply. "The happiness," she said, and against her will her voice trembled and faltered—"the happiness that a true, earnest love alone can give—which I have received joyously into my heart as a gift from God."

The prince laughed aloud, but his face had a wild, despairing expression, and his hands clasped the chair more firmly.

"I do not understand your holy, pious words. What do they mean? What do you wish to say?"

"They mean that I now love so truly and so earnestly that I have promised to become the wife of the man I love," said Louise, with forced gayety.

The prince uttered a wild cry, and raised his hands as if to curse the one who had wounded him so painfully.

"If this is true," he said, in a deep, hollow voice—"if this is true, I despise, I hate you, and they are right who call you a heartless coquette."

"Ah, my prince, you insult me," cried Louise.

"I insult you!" he said, with a wild laugh; "verily, I believe this woman has the effrontery to reproach me—I who believed in and defended her against every accusation—I that had the courage to love and trust, when all others distrusted and despised her. Yes, madame, I loved you: I saw in you a goddess, where others saw only a coquette. I adored you as an innocent sacrifice to envy and malice; I saw a martyr's crown upon your brow, and wished to change it for the myrtle-crown of marriage. And my love and hopes are dust and ashes; it is enough to drive me mad—enough to stifle me with rage and shame." Carried away by passion, the prince ran wildly through the saloon, gasping for air, struggling for composure, and now and then uttering words of imprecation and despair.

Louise waited, in silence and resignation, the end of this stormy crisis. She questioned her heart if this bitter hour was not sufficient atonement for all her faults and follies; if the agony she now suffered did not wipe out and extirpate the past.

The prince still paced the room violently. Suddenly, as if a new thought had seized him, he remained standing in the middle of the saloon, and looked at Louise with a strangely altered countenance. She had forgotten for a moment the part she was condemned to play, and leaned, pale and sad, against the window.

Perhaps he heard her sorrowful sighs—perhaps he saw her tears as they rolled one by one from her eyes, and fell like pearls upon her small white hands.

Anger disappeared from his face, his brow cleared, and as he approached Louise his eyes sparkled with another and milder fire.

"Louise," he said, softly, and his voice, which had before raged like a stormy wind, was now mild and tender—"Louise, I have divined your purpose—I know all now. At first, I did not understand your words; in my folly and jealousy I misconceived your meaning; you only wished to try me, to see if my love was armed and strong, if it was as bold and faithful as I have sworn it to be. Well, I stood the test badly, was weak and faint-hearted; but forgive me—forgive me, Louise, and strengthen my heart by confidence and faith in me."

He tried to take her hand, but she withdrew it.

"Must I repeat to your highness what I have said before? I do not understand you. What do you mean?"

"Ah," said the prince, "you are again my naughty, sportive Louise. Well, then, I will explain. Did you not say that you now love so truly, that you have promised to become the wife of the man you love?"

"Yes, I said that, your highness."

"And I," said the prince, seizing both her hands and gazing at her ardently—"I was so short-sighted, so ungrateful, as not to understand you. The many sorrows and vexations I suffer away from you have dimmed my eyes and prevented me from seeing what is written with golden letters upon your smiling lips and beaming eyes. Ah, Louise, I thank you for your precious words, at last you are captured, at last you have resolved to become the wife of him who adores you. I thank you, Louise, I thank you, and I swear that no earthly pomp or power could make me as proud and happy as this assurance of your love."

Louise gazed into his beautiful, smiling face with terror.

"Ah, my prince, my words have not the meaning you imagine. I spoke the simple truth. My heart has made its choice—since yesterday, I am the betrothed wife of Captain du Trouffle."

"That is not true," cried the prince, casting her hands violently from him. "You are very cruel today; you torture me with your fearful jests."

"No, your highness, I speak the truth. I am the betrothed of Captain du Trouffle."

"Since yesterday you are the betrothed of Captain du Trouffle!" repeated the prince, staring at her wildly. "And you say you love him, Louise?"

"Yes, your highness, I love him," said Louise, with a faint smile.

"It is impossible," cried the prince; "it is not true."

"And why should I deceive your highness?"

"Why?—ah, I understand all. Oh, Louise, my poor darling, how short-sighted I have been! Why did I not immediately suspect my brother?—he has spies to watch all my movements; they have at last discovered my love for you. Pollnitz, who would do any thing for gold, has betrayed us to the king, who condemns me to marry according to my rank, and, to carry out his purpose surely, he now forces you to marry. Oh, Louise, say that this is so; acknowledge that the power of the king, and not your own heart, forced you to this engagement. It is impossible, it cannot be that you have forgotten the vows that we exchanged scarcely two weeks ago. It cannot be that you look upon the heart that loved you so deeply, so purely, as an idle plaything, to be thrown away so lightly! No, no, Louise, I have seen often in your beaming eyes, your eloquent smiles, I have felt in your soft and tender tones, that you loved me fondly; and now in your pale, sad face I see that you love me still, and that it is the king who wishes to separate us. My poor, lovely child, you have been intimidated; you think that my brother, who reigns supreme over millions, will yield to no obstacle, that it is vain to resist him. But you are mistaken, Louise; you have forgotten that I am Frederick's brother, that the proud, unconquerable blood of the Hohenzollerns flows also in my veins. Let my brother try to force me to his purpose; I shall be no weak tool in his hands. You had not firm confidence in your lover, Louise; you did not know that I would resign cheerfully rank and all family ties for your sake; you did not know that I had sworn to marry only the woman I love. This I must do to satisfy my heart and my honor, and also to show the king that Prince Henry is a free man. Now tell me, Louise, if I have not divined all. Is not this the king's cruel work? Ah, you do not answer, you are silent. I understand—the king has made you swear not to betray him. Now look at me, Louise; make me a sign with your hand, tell me with your eyes, and I will comprehend you—I will take you in my arms and carry you to the altar. My God! Louise do you not see that I am waiting for this sign?—that you are torturing me?"

Louise raised her head, her heart was melting within her; she forgot her terror, and was ready to resist God, the king, and the whole world, to grasp the noble and unselfish love that the prince offered her. But her glance fell involuntarily upon the curtain, behind which the king stood, and it seemed to her as if she saw the angry, burning eyes of Frederick threatening to destroy her. She remembered her daughter, Fritz Wendel, and the world's mocking laughter, and was overcome.

"You are still silent," said the prince; "you give me neither sign nor glance."

Louise felt as if an iron hand was tearing her heart asunder.

"I really am at a loss what more to say or do," she said, in a careless tone, that made her own heart shudder. "It pleases your highness to make a jest of what I say. I am innocent, my prince, of any double meaning. Five weeks have passed since I saw you—I believed you had forgotten me; I did not reproach you, neither was I in despair. I soon found that it was stupid and dreary to have my heart unoccupied, and I sought for and soon found a lover, to whom my heart became a willing captive. Therefore, when Captain Trouffle pleaded earnestly for my hand, I had not the courage to say no. This is my only crime, your highness. I was not cruel to myself; I received the happiness that was offered. I have been called a coquette, my prince; it is time to bind myself in marriage bonds, and show the world that love can make an honest woman of me. Can your highness blame me for this?"

The prince listened with breathless attention; gradually his countenance changed, the color faded from his cheeks, the light from his eyes; a smile was still on his lips, but it was cold and mocking; his eyes burned with anger and contempt.

"No, madame," he said, with calm, proud indifference, "I do not blame you—I praise, I congratulate you. Captain du Trouffle is a most fortunate man—he will possess a most beautiful wife. When will this happy ceremony be performed?"

Madame von Kleist was unable to reply. She gazed with wild terror into his cold, iron face—she listened with horror to that voice, whose mild, soft tone had become suddenly so harsh, so stern.

The prince repeated his question, and his tone was harder and more imperious.

"The day is not fixed," said Louise; "we must first obtain the king's consent to our marriage."

"I shall take care it does not fail you," said the prince, quietly.

"I will strengthen your petition to the king. Now, madame, you must forgive me for leaving you. Many greetings to your betrothed—I shall be introduced to him to-morrow at the parade. Farewell, madame!"

The prince made a slight bow, and, without glancing at her again, left the room slowly and proudly.

Louise gazed after him with mournful eyes, but he did not see it; he did not see how she fell, as if broken, to the floor, as if struck by lightning; and when the door closed on him she held her hands to Heaven pleadingly for mercy and forgiveness.

The portiere now opened, and the king entered; his countenance was pale, his eyes tearful, but they sparkled with anger when he saw Louise upon the floor. For him she was but a heartless coquette, and he was angry with her because of the suffering she had caused his brother, for whom he felt the deepest pity and compassion.

But that was now past; the brother could weep a tear of pity, the king must be firm and relentless.

As he approached her, she raised herself from the ground and made a profound and ceremonious bow.

"You have repaired much of the evil you have done, madame," said the king, sternly. "You have played a dishonorable game with my brother. You enticed him to love you."

"I think I have atoned, sire," said Louise, faintly; "the prince no longer loves but despises me. Your commands are fulfilled to the letter, and I now beg your majesty's permission to withdraw."

"Go, madame; you have done your duty to-day, and I will also do mine. I shall not forget what I promised you when you are Madame du Trouffle. We will forget all the faults of Madame von Kleist."

He dismissed her with a slight bow, and gazed after her until she had disappeared.

At this moment, a heavy fall was heard in the antechamber. The door opened immediately, and the pale, disturbed face of Pollnitz appeared.

"What is the matter, Pollnitz?" asked the king, hastily.

"Oh, sire, poor Prince Henry has fainted."

The king was startled, and stepped quickly to the door, but he remained standing there until his features resumed their calm expression.

"He will recover," he said—"he will recover, for he is a man; in my youthful days I often fainted, but I recovered."

CHAPTER X
THE CONQUERED

Painful and bitter were the days for Henry that followed his first disappointment. He passed them in rigid seclusion, in his lonely chambers; he would see no one, no cheerful word or gay laughter was allowed in his presence. The servants looked at him sorrowfully; and when the prince appeared at the parade the day after his painful interview with Louise, even the king found him so pale and suffering, he begged him to take a week's leave and strengthen and improve his health.

The prince smiled painfully at the king's proposition, but he accepted his leave of absence, and withdrew to the solitude of his rooms. His heart was wounded unto death, his soul was agonized. Youth soon laid its healing balm upon his wounds and closed them; anger and contempt dried his tears, and soothed the anguish of his heart.

The king was right when he said of his brother, "He is a man, and will recover." He did recover, and these days of suffering made a man of him; his brow, once so clear and youthful, had received its first mark of sorrow; the lines of his face were harsh and stern, his features sharper and more decided. He had experienced his first disappointment—it had nerved and strengthened him.

Before his eight days' leave of absence had expired, his door was again open to his circle of friends and confidants.

His first invited guest was the grand chamberlain, Baron Pollnitz. The prince welcomed him with a bright and cheerful face.

"Do you know why I wished to see you?" he asked. "You must tell me the chronique scandaleuse of our most honorable and virtuous city. Commence immediately. What is the on dit of the day?"

"Ah," sighed Pollnitz, "life is now stupid, dull, and monotonous. As you say, every one has become most honorable and virtuous. No scandals or piquant adventures occur, baptisms, marriages, and burials are the only events. This is really a miserable existence; for as I do not wish to be baptized or to marry, and as I am not yet ready for burial, I really do not know why I exist."

"But those that are married and baptized, doubtless know why they exist," said the prince, smiling. "Tell me something of this happy class. Whose, for example, is the latest marriage?"

"The latest marriage?" said Pollnitz, hesitating—"before answering, I must allow myself to ask after the condition of your heart. Does it still suffer?"

"No," cried the prince, "it does not suffer; it received a heavy shower of cold water, and was cured instantly."

"I rejoice to hear it, your highness, and congratulate you on your recovery, for truly there is no more painful disease than a suffering heart."

"I told you that I had recovered fully; tell me, therefore, your news without hesitation. You spoke of a marriage. Who were the happy lovers?"

"Your highness, Madame von Kleist has married," murmured Pollnitz.

The prince received this blow without betraying the slightest emotion.

"When did the marriage take place?" he asked, with perfect composure.

"Yesterday; and I assure your highness that I never saw a happier or more brilliant bride. Love has transformed her into a blushing, timid maiden."

Prince Henry pressed his hand upon his heart with a quick, unconscious movement.

"I can well imagine that she was beautiful," said he, controlling his voice with a great effort. "Madame von Kleist is happy, and happiness always beautifies. And the bridegroom, M. du Trouffle, was he also handsome and happy?"

"Your highness knows the name of the bride-groom," said Pollnitz, appearing astonished.

"Yes, Madame von Kleist told me herself when she announced her approaching marriage. But I am not acquainted with Du Trouffle—is he handsome?"

"Handsome and amiable, your highness, and besides, a very good officer. The king gave him, as a wedding present, a major's commission."

"Then the beautiful Louise is now Mrs Major du Trouffle," said the prince, with a troubled smile. "Were you present at the wedding?"

"Yes, in the name of the king."

"Did she speak the decisive Yes, the vow of faith and obedience, with earnestness and confidence? Did she not blush, or droop her eyelids in doing so?"

"Oh, no; she smiled as if entranced, and raised her eyes to heaven, as if praying for God's blessing upon her vows."

"One thing more," said the prince, fixing his large, gray eyes with a searching expression upon Pollnitz—"what is said of me? Am I regarded as a rejected lover, or as a faithless one; for doubtless all Berlin knows of my love for this lady, you having been our confidant."

"Oh, my prince, that is a hard insinuation," said Pollnitz, sadly.

"Your highness cannot really believe that—"

"No protestations, I pray you," interrupted the prince, "I believe I know you thoroughly, but I am not angry with you nor do I reproach you: you are a courtier, and one of the best and rarest type; you have intellect and knowledge, much experience and savoir vivre; I could desire no better company than yourself; but for one moment cast aside your character as a courtier, and tell me the truth: what does the world say of this marriage in regard to me?"

"Your highness desires me to tell you the truth?"

"Yes, I do."

"Now the important moment has come," thought Pollnitz. "Now, if I am adroit, I believe I can obtain the payment of my debts."

"Well, then, your highness," said Pollnitz, in answer to the prince, "I will tell you the truth, even should I incur your displeasure. I fear, my prince, you are regarded as a rejected lover, and Madame du Trouffle has succeeded in throwing a holy lustre around her beautiful brow. It is said that she refused your dishonorable proposals, and preferred being the virtuous wife of a major, to becoming the mistress of a prince."

"Go on," said the prince, hastily, as Pollnitz ceased, and looked searchingly at him. "What do they say of me?"

"That you are in despair, and that you have retired to your chambers to weep and mourn over your lost love."

"Ah, they say that, do they?" cried the prince, with flashing eyes and darkened brow; "well, I will show this credulous world that they are mistaken. Is the king in Sans-Souci?"

"Yes, your highness."

"Well, go to him, and announce my visit; I will follow you on foot."

"We have won the day," cried Pollnitz, as he approached the king; "the prince desires to make you a visit. He will be here immediately."

"Do you know what my brother wishes of me?" asked the king.

"I do not know, but I suspect, sire. I think he wishes to marry, in order to pique his faithless sweetheart."

"Go and receive the prince, and conduct him to me; then remain in the antechamber, and await until I call."

When Pollnitz left, the king seized his flute hastily aim began to play a soft, melting adagio. He was still playing, when the door opened, and the prince was announced. Henry stood in the doorway, and made the king a ceremonious bow. The king continued to play. The low, pleading notes of the flute floated softly through the room; they touched the heart of the prince, and quieted its wild, stormy beating.

Was that the king's intention, or did he intend to harmonize his own spirit before speaking to his brother? Perhaps both, for Frederick's glance softened, and his face assumed a kind and mild expression.

When the adagio was finished, the king laid his flute aside and approached the prince.

"Forgive me, brother," he said, offering his hand—"forgive me for keeping you waiting, I always like to conclude what I commence. Now, I am entirely at your service, and as I am unfortunately not accustomed to receive such friendly visits from you, I must ask you what brings you to me, and how I can serve you?"

The fierce, violent nature of the prince slumbered but lightly. The king's words aroused it, and made his pulse and heart beat stormily.

"How you can serve me, my brother?" he said, hastily. "I will tell you, and truthfully, sire."

The king raised his head, and glanced angrily at the burning face of the prince.

"I am not accustomed to have my words repeated, and all find that out here to their cost," he said, sternly.

"Have the goodness, then, to tell me why you have pursued me so long and unrelentingly? What have I done to deserve your displeasure and such bitter humiliations?"

"Rather ask me what you have done to deserve my love and confidence," said the king, sternly. "I refer you to your own heart for an answer."

"Ah, your majesty promised to answer my questions, and now you evade them, but I will reply frankly. I have done nothing to deserve your love, but also nothing to make me unworthy of it. Why are you, who are so good and kind to all others, so stern and harsh with me?"

"I will tell you the truth," said the king, earnestly. "You have deserved my displeasure, you have desired to be a free man, to cast aside the yoke that Providence placed upon you, you had the grand presumption to dare to be the master of your own actions."

"And does your majesty desire and expect me to resign this most natural of human rights?" said the prince, angrily.

"Yes, I desire and expect it. I can truthfully say that I have given my brothers a good example in this particular."

"But you did not do this willingly. You were cruelly forced to submission, and you now wish to drive us to an extremity you have, doubtlessly, long since forgotten. Now, you suffered and struggled before declaring yourself conquered."

"No," said the king, softly, "I have not forgotten. I still feel the wound in my soul, and at times it burns."

"And yet, my brother?"

"And yet I will have no pity with you. I say to you, as my father said to me: 'You must submit; you are a prince, and I am your king!' I have long since acknowledged that my father was right in his conduct to me. I was not only a disobedient son, but a rebellious subject. I richly deserved to mount the scaffold with Katte."

"Ah, my brother, there was a time when you wept for this faithful and unfortunate friend," cried the prince, reproachfully.

"The sons of kings have not the right to choose their own path, destiny has marked it out for them; they must follow it without wavering. I neither placed the crown upon my head, nor the yoke upon your neck. We must bear them patiently, as God and Providence have ordained, and wear them with grace and dignity. You, my brother, have acted like a wild horse of the desert—I have drawn the reins tight, that is all!"

"You have caught, bound, and tamed me," said the prince, with a faint smile; "only I feel that the bit still pains, and that my limbs still tremble. But I am ready to submit, and I came to tell you so. You desire me to marry, I consent; but I hold you responsible for the happiness of this marriage. At God's throne, I will call you to justify yourself, and there we will speak as equals, as man to man. What right had you to rob me of my most holy and beautiful possession? What right have you to lay a heavy chain on heart and hand, that love will not help me to bear? I hold you responsible for my miserable life, my shattered hopes. Will you accept these conditions? Do you still wish me to marry?"

"I accept the conditions," said the king, solemnly. "I desire you to marry."

"I presume your majesty has chosen a bride for me?"

"You are right, mon cher frere. I have selected the Princess Wilhelmina, daughter of Prince Max, of Hesse-Cassel. She not only brings you a fortune, but youth, beauty, and amiability."

"I thank you, sire," said the prince, coldly and formally. "I would marry her if she were ugly, old, and unamiable. But is it allowed me to add one condition?"

"Speak, my brother, I am listening."

The prince did not answer immediately; he breathed quickly and heavily, and a glowing red suffused his pale, trembling face.

"Speak, my brother. Name your conditions," said the king.

"Well, then, so be it. My first condition is that I may be allowed to have a brilliant wedding. I wish to invite not only the entire court, but a goodly number of Berliners; I desire all Berlin to take part in my happiness, and to convince every one, by my gay demeanor and my entertainment, that I joyfully accept my bride, the princess."

The king's eyes rested sorrowfully upon his brother's countenance. He fully understood the emotions of his heart, and knew that his brother wished to wound and humiliate his faithless sweetheart by his marriage; that Henry only submitted to his wishes because his proud heart rebelled at the thought of being pitied as a rejected lover. But he was considerate, and would not let it appear that he understood him.

"I agree to this first proposition," said the king, after a pause, "and I hope you will allow me to be present at this beautiful fete, and convince Berlin that we are in hearty unison. Have you no other conditions?"

"Yes, one more."

"What is it?"

"That my marriage shall take place, at the latest, in a month."

"You will thus fulfil my particular and personal wish," said the king, smiling. "I am anxious to have this marriage over, for, after the gayeties,

I wish to leave Berlin. All the arrangements and contracts are completed, and I think now there is no obstacle in the way of the marriage. Have you another wish, my brother?"

"No, sire."

"Then allow me to beg you to grant me a favor. I wish to leave a kind remembrance of this eventful hour in your heart, and I therefore give you a small memento of the same. Will you accept my castle of Rheinsberg, with all its surroundings, as a present from me? Will you grant me this pleasure, my brother?"

The king offered his hand, with a loving smile, to Henry, and received with apparent pleasure his ardent thanks.

"I chose Rheinsberg," he said, kindly, "not because it is my favorite palace, and I have passed many pleasant and happy days there, but because none of my other palaces are so appropriate for a prince who is discontented with his king. I have made that experience myself, and I give you Rheinsberg, as my father gave it to me. Go to Rheinsberg when you are angry with me and the world; there you can pass the first months of your marriage, and God grant it may be a happy one!"

The prince answered him with a cold smile, and begged leave to withdraw, that he might make the necessary preparations for his wedding. "We will both make our preparations," said the king, as he bade the prince farewell—"you with your major-domo, and I with Baron Pollnitz, whom I shall send as ambassador to Cassel."

CHAPTER XI
THE TRAVELLING MUSICIANS

The feasts, illuminations, and balls given in honor of the newly-married couple, Henry and his wife, the Princess Wilhelmina, were at an end. The prince and his followers had withdrawn to Rheinsberg, and many were the rumors in Berlin of the brilliant feasts with which he welcomed his beautiful bride. She was truly lovely, and the good Berliners, who had received her with such hearty greetings when she appeared with the prince on the balcony, or showed herself to the people in an open carriage, declared there could be no happier couple than the prince and his wife; they declared that the large, dark eyes of the princess rested upon the prince with inexpressible tenderness, and that the prince always returned her glance with a joyous smile. It was therefore decided that the prince was a happy husband, and the blessings of the Berliners followed the charming princess to Rheinsberg, where the young couple were to pass their honeymoon.

While the prince was giving splendid fetes, and seeking distraction, and hoping to forget his private griefs, or perhaps wishing to deceive the world as to his real feelings, the king left Sans-Souci, to commence one of his customary military inspection trips. But he did not go to Konigsberg, as was supposed; and if Trenck really had the intention of murdering him during his sojourn there, it was rendered impossible by the change in the king's plans. Frederick made a tour in his Rhine provinces. At Cleves he dismissed his followers, and they returned to Berlin.

The king declared he needed rest, and wished to pass a few days in undisturbed quiet at the castle of Moyland.

No one accompanied him but Colonel Balby, his intimate friend, and his cabinet-hussar, Deesen. The king was in an uncommonly good humor, and his eyes sparkled with delight. After a short rest in his chamber, he desired to see Colonel Balby.

To his great astonishment, the colonel found him searching through a trunk, which contained a few articles of clothing little calculated to arrest the attention of a king.

"Balby," said the king, solemnly, but with a roguish sparkle of the eye, "I wish to present you this plain brown suit. I owe you a reward for your hearty friendship and your faithful services. This is a princely gift. Take it as a mark of my grateful regard. That you may be convinced, Balby, that I have long been occupied in preparing this surprise for you, I inform you that these rich articles were made secretly for you in Berlin, by your tailor; I packed them myself, and brought them here for you. Accept them, then, my friend, and wear them in memory of Frederick."

With a solemn bow, the king offered Balby the clothes.

The colonel received this strange present with an astonished and somewhat confused countenance.

The king laughed merrily. "What," he said, pathetically, "are you not contented with the favor I have shown you?"

Balby knew by the comic manner of the king that the sombre suit hid a secret, and he thought it wise to allow the king to take his own time for explanation.

"Sire," he said, emphatically, "content is not the word to express my rapture. I am enthusiastic, speechless at this unheard-of favor. I am filled with profound gratitude to your majesty for having in vented a new costume for me, whose lovely color will make me appear like a large coffee-bean, and make all the coffee sisters adore me."

The king was highly amused. "This dress certainly has the power of enchantment. When Colonel Balby puts on these clothes he will be invisible, but he shall not undergo this transformation alone. See, here is another suit, exactly like yours, and this is mine. When I array myself in it, I am no longer the king of Prussia, but a free, happy man."

"Ah, you are speaking of a disguise," cried the colonel.

"Yes, we will amuse ourselves by playing the role of common men for a while, and wander about unnoticed and undisturbed. Are you agreed, Balby, or do you love your colonel's uniform better than your freedom?"

"Am I agreed, sire?" cried the colonel; "I am delighted with this genial thought."

"Then take your dress, friend, and put it on. But stay. Did you bring your violin with you, as I told you?"

"Yes, sire."

"Well, then, when you are dressed, put your violin in a case, and with the case under your arm, and a little money in your pocket, go to the pavilion at the farthest end of the garden; there I will meet you. Now hasten, friend, we have no time to lose."

According to the king's orders, Colonel Balby dressed and went to the pavilion. He did not find the king, but two strange men there. One of them had on a brown coat, the color of his own, ornamented with large buttons of mother-of-pearl; black pantaloons, and shoes with large buckles, set with dull white stones; the lace on his sleeves and vest was very coarse. He wore a three-cornered hat, without ornament; from under the hat fell long, brown, unpowdered hair.

Behind this stranger there stood another, in plain, simple clothes; under one arm he carried a small bag, and under the other a case that contained either a yard-stick or a flute. He returned the colonel's salutation with a grimace and a profound bow. A short pause ensued, then the supposed strangers laughed heartily and exclaimed:

"Do you not know us, Balby?"

Their voices started the colonel, and he stepped back.

"Sire, it is yourself."

"Yes, it is I, Frederick—not the king. Yes, I am Frederick, and this capital servant is my good Deesen, who has sworn solemnly not to betray our incognito, and to give no one reason to suspect his high dignity as royal cabinet-hussar. For love of us he will, for a few days, be the servant of two simple, untitled musicians, who are travelling around the world, seeking their fortunes, but who, unfortunately, have no letters of recommendation."

"But who will recommend themselves by their talents and accomplishments."

The king laughed aloud. "Balby, you forget that you are a poor musician, chatting with your comrade. Truly your courtly bow suits your dress as little as a lace veil would a beggar's attire; you must lay your fine manners aside for a short time, for, with them, you would appear to the village beauties we may meet like a monkey, and they would laugh at instead of kissing you."

"So we are to meet country beauties," said Colonel Balby, no longer able to suppress his curiosity. "Tell me, sire, where are we going, and what are we going to do? I shall die of curiosity."

"Make an effort to die," said the king, gayly; "you will find it is not so easy to do as you imagine. But I will torture you no longer. You ask what we are going to do. Well, we are going to amuse ourselves and seek adventures. You ask where we are going. Ask that question of the sparrow that sits on the house-top—ask where it is going, and what is the aim of its journey. It will reply, the next bush, the nearest tree, the topmost bough of a weeping willow, which stands on a lonely grave; the mast of a ship, sailing on the wide sea; or the branch of a noble beech, waving before the window of a beautiful maiden. I am as incapable of telling you the exact aim and end of our journey, friend, as that little bird would be. We are as free as the birds of the air. Come! come! let us fly, for see, the little sparrow has flown—let us follow it."

And with a beaming smile illuminating his countenance, like a ray of the morning sun, the king took the arm of his friend, and followed by his servant and cabinet-hussar, Deesen, left the pavilion.

As they stood at the little gate of the garden, the king said to Deesen,

"You must be for us the angel with the flaming sword, and open the gates of paradise, but not to cast us out."

Deesen opened the gate, and our adventurers entered "the wide, wide world."

"Let us stand here a few moments," said the king, as his glance rested upon the green fields spread far and wide around him. "How great and beautiful the world appears to-day! Observe Nature's grand silence, yet the air is full of a thousand voices, and the white clouds wandering dreamily in the blue heavens above, are they not the misty veils with which the gods of Olympus conceal their charms?"

"Ah! sire," said Balby, with a loving glance at the king's handsome face—"ah, sire, my eyes have no time to gaze at Nature's charms, they are occupied with yourself. When I look upon you, I feel that man is indeed made in the image of God."

"Were I a god, I should not be content to resemble this worn, faded face. Come, now, let us be off! Give me your instrument, Deesen, I will carry it. Now I look like a travelling apprentice seeking his fortune. The world is all before him where to choose his place of rest, and Providence his guide. I envy him. He is a free man!"

"Truly, these poor apprentices would not believe that a king was envying them their fate," said Balby, laughing.

"Still they are to be envied," said the king, "for they are free. No, no, at present I envy no one, the world and its sunshine belong to me. We will go to Amsterdam, and enjoy the galleries and museums."

"I thank your majesty," said Balby, laughing, "you have saved my life. I should have died of curiosity if you had not spoken. Now, I feel powerful and strong, and can keep pace with your majesty's wandering steps."

Silently they walked on until they reached a sign-post.

"We are now on the border—let us bid farewell to the Prussian colors, we see them for the last time. Sire, we will greet them with reverence."

He took off his hat and bowed lowly before the black and white colors of Prussia, a greeting that Deesen imitated with the fervor of a patriot.

The king did not unite in their enthusiasm; he was writing with his stick upon the ground.

"Come here, Balby, and read this," he said, pointing to the lines he had traced. "Can you read them?"

"Certainly," said Balby, "the words are, 'majesty' and 'sire.'"

"So they are, friend. I leave these two words on the borders of Prussia; perhaps on our return we may find and resume them. But as long as we are on the soil of Holland there must be no majesty, no sire."

"What, then, must I call my king?"

"You must call him friend, voila tout."

"And I?" asked Deesen, respectfully. "Will your majesty be so gracious as to tell me your name?"

"I am Mr. Zoller, travelling musician, and should any one ask you what I want in Amsterdam, tell them I intend giving a concert. En avant, mes amis. There lies the first small village of Holland, in an hour we shall be there, and then we will take the stage and go a little into the interior. En avant, en avant!"

CHAPTER XII
TRAVELLING ADVENTURES

The stage stood before the tavern at Grave, and awaited its passengers. The departure of the stage was an important occurrence to the inhabitants of the little town—an occurrence that disturbed the monotony of their lives for a few moments, and showed them at least now and then a new face, that gave them something to think of, and made them dream of the far-off city where the envied travellers were going.

Today all Grave was in commotion and excitement. The strangers had arrived at the post-house, and after partaking of an excellent dinner, engaged three seats in the stage. The good people of Grave hoped to see three strange faces looking out of the stage window; many were the surmises of their destiny and their possible motives for travelling. They commenced these investigations while the strangers were still with them.

A man had seen them enter the city, dusty and exhausted, and he declared that the glance which the two men in brown coats had cast at his young wife, who had come to the window at his call, was very bold—yes, even suspicious, and it seemed very remarkable to him that such plain, ordinary looking wanderers should have a servant, for, doubtless, the man walking behind them, carrying the very small carpet-bag, was their servant; but, truly, he appeared to be a proud person, and had the haughty bearing of a general or a field-marshal, he would not even return the friendly greetings of the people he passed. His masters could not be distinguished or rich, for both of them carried a case under their arms. What could be in those long cases, what secret was hidden there? Perhaps they held pistols, and the good people of Grave would have to deal with robbers or murderers. The appearance of the strangers was wild and bold enough to allow of the worst suspicions.

The whole town, as before mentioned, was in commotion, and all were anxious to see the three strangers, about whom there was certainly something mysterious. They had the manners and bearing of noblemen, but were dressed like common men.

A crowd of idlers had assembled before the post-house, whispering and staring at the windows of the guests' rooms. At last their curiosity was about to be gratified, at last the servant appeared with the little carpet-bag, and placed it in the stage, and returned for the two cases, whose contents they would so greedily have known. The postilion blew his horn, the moment of departure had arrived.

A murmur was heard through the crowd, the strangers appeared, they approached the stage, and with such haughty and commanding glances that the men nearest them stepped timidly back.

The postilion sounded his horn again, the strangers were entering the stage. At the door stood the postmaster, and behind him his wife, the commanding postmistress.

"Niclas," she whispered, "I must and will know who these strangers are. Go and demand their passports."

The obedient Niclas stepped out and cried in a thundering voice to the postilion, who was just about to start, to wait. Stepping to the stage, he opened the door.

"Your passports, gentlemen," he said, roughly. "You forgot to show me your passports."

The curious observers breathed more freely, and nodded encouragingly to the daring postmaster.

"You rejoice," murmured his wife, who was still standing in the door, from whence she saw all that passed, and seemed to divine the thoughts of her gaping friends—"you rejoice, but you shall know nothing. I shall not satisfy your curiosity."

Mr. Niclas still stood at the door of the stage. His demand had not been attended to; he repeated it for the third time.

"Is it customary here to demand passports of travellers?" asked a commanding voice from the stage.

Niclas, and taking the two mysterious cases from the stage, he placed them before the strangers.

"Let us go into the house," whispered the king to his friends. "We must make bonne mine a mauvais jeu," and he approached the door of the house—there stood the wife of the postmaster, with sparkling eyes and a malicious grin.

"The postilion is going, and you will lose your money," she said, "they never return money when once they have it."

"Ah! I thought that was only a habit of the church," said the king, laughing. "Nevertheless, the postmaster can keep what he has. Will you have the kindness to show me a room, where I can open my bag at leisure, and send some coffee and good wine to us?"

There was something so commanding in the king's voice, so imposing in his whole appearance, that even the all-conquering Madame Niclas felt awed, and she silently stepped forward and showed him her best room. The servant followed with the two cases and the bag, and laid them upon the table, then placed himself at the door.

"Now, madame, leave us," ordered the king, "and do as I told you."

Madame Niclas left, and the gentlemen were once more alone.

"Now, what shall we do?" said the king, smilingly. "I believe there is danger of our wonderful trip falling through."

"It is only necessary for your majesty to make yourself known to the postmaster," said Colonel Balby.

"And if he will not believe me, this fripon who declares that no one could tell by my appearance whether I was a rascal or not, this dull-eyed simpleton, who will not see the royal mark upon my brow, which my courtiers see so plainly written there? No, no, my friend, that is not the way. We have undertaken to travel as ordinary men—we must now see how common men get through the world. It is necessary to show the police that we are at least honest men. Happily, I believe I have the means to do so at hand. Open our ominous bag, friend Balby, I think you will discover my portfolio, and in it a few blank passes, and my state seal."

Colonel Balby did as the king ordered, and drew from the bag the portfolio, with its precious contents.

The king bade Balby sit down and fill up the blanks at his dictation.

The pass was drawn up for the two brothers, Frederick and Henry Zoller, accompanied by their servant, with the intention of travelling through Holland.

The king placed his signature under this important document.

"Now, it is only necessary to put the state seal under it, and we shall be free; but how will we get a light?"

"I cannot tell who is a rascal, you may be one for aught I know."

Balby uttered an angry exclamation and stepped nearer to the daring postmaster, while his servant shook his fist threateningly at Niclas.

The king dispelled their anger with a single glance.

"Sir," he said to Niclas, "God made my face, and it is not my fault if it does not please you, but concerning our passports, they are lying well preserved in my carpet-bag. I should think that would suffice you."

"No, that does not suffice me," screamed Niclas. "Show me your passports if I am to believe that you are not vagabonds."

"You dare to call us vagabonds?" cried the king, whose patience now also appeared exhausted, and whose clear brow was slightly clouded.

"The police consider everyone criminal until he has proved he is not so," said Niclas, emphatically.

The king's anger was already subdued.

"In the eyes of the police, criminality is then the normal condition of mankind," he said, smilingly.

"Sir, you have no right to question the police so pointedly," said Niclas, sternly. "You are here to be questioned, and not to question."

The king laughingly arrested the uplifted arm of his companion.

"Mon Dieu," he murmured, "do you not see that this is amusing me highly? Ask, sir, I am ready to answer."

"Have you a pass?"

"Yes, sir."

"Then give it to me to vise."

"To do so, I should have to open my bag, and that would be very inconvenient, but, if the law absolutely demands it, I will do it."

"The law demands it."

The king motioned to his servant, and ordered him to carry the bag into the house.

"Why this delay—why this unnecessary loss of time?" asked Niclas. "The postilion can wait no longer. If he arrives too late at the next station, he will be fined."

"I will not wait another minute," cried the postilion, determinately. "get in, or I shall start without you."

"Show me your passports, and then get in," cried Niclas.

The strangers appeared confused and undecided. Niclas looked triumphantly at his immense crowd of listeners, who were gazing at him with amazement, awaiting in breathless stillness the unravelling of this scene.

"Get in, or I shall start," repeated the postilion.

"Give me your passports, or I will not let you go!" screamed "We can demand them if we wish to do so."

"And why do you wish it now?" said the same voice.

"I wish it simply because I wish it," was the reply.

A stern face now appeared at the door, looking angrily at the postmaster.

"Think what you say, sir, and be respectful."

"Silence!" interrupted the one who had first spoken. "Do not let us make an unnecessary disturbance, mon ami. Why do you wish to see our passports, sir?"

"Why?" asked Niclas, who was proud to play so distinguished a part before his comrades—"you wish to know why I desire to see your passports? Well, then, because you appear to me to be suspicious characters."

A gay laugh was heard from the stage. "Why do you suspect us?"

"Because I never trust people travelling without baggage," was the laconic reply.

"Bravo! well answered," cried the crowd, and even Madame Niclas was surprised to see her husband show such daring courage.

"We need no baggage. We are travelling musicians, going to Amsterdam."

"Travelling musicians All the more reason for mistrusting you; no good was ever heard of wandering musicians."

"You are becoming impertinent, sir," and Balby, the tallest and youngest of the two friends, sprang from the stage, while the servant swung himself from the box, where he was sitting with the postilion, and with an enraged countenance placed himself beside his master.

"If you dare to speak another insulting word, you are lost," cried Balby.

A hand was laid on his shoulder, and a voice murmured in his ear:

"Do not compromise us."

The king now also left the stage, and tried to subdue the anger of his companion.

"Pardon, sir, the violence of my friend," said the king, with an ironical smile, as he bowed to the postmaster. "We are not accustomed to being questioned and suspected in this manner, and I can assure you that, although we are travelling musicians, as it pleased you to say, we are honest people, and have played before kings and queens."

"If you are honest, show me your passports; no honest man travels without one!"

"It appears to me that no rascal should travel without one," said the king. "I will obtain one immediately," said Balby, hastening to the door.

The king held him back. "My brother, you are very innocent and thoughtless. You forget entirely that we are suspected criminals. Should we demand a light, and immediately appear with our passes, do you not believe that this dragon of a postmaster would immediately think that we had written them ourselves, and put a forged seal under them?"

"How, then, are we to get a light?" said Balby, confused.

The king thought a moment, then laughed gayly.

"I have found a way," he said; "go down into the dining-room, where I noticed an eternal lamp burning, not to do honor to the Mother of God, but to smokers; light your cigar and bring it here. I will light the sealing-wax by it, and we will have the advantage of drowning the smell of the wax with the smoke."

Balby flew away, and soon returned with the burning cigar; the king lit the sealing-wax, and put the seal under the passport.

"This will proclaim us free from all crime. Now, brother Henry, call the worthy postmaster."

When Niclas received the passport from the king's hand his countenance cleared, and he made the two gentlemen a graceful bow, and begged them to excuse the severity that his duty made necessary.

"We have now entirely convinced you that we are honest people," said the king, smiling, "and you will forgive us that we have so little baggage."

"Well, I understand," said Mr. Niclas, confusedly, "musicians are seldom rich, but live from hand to mouth, and must thank God if their clothes are good and clean. Yours are entirely new, and you need no baggage."

The king laughed merrily. "Can we now go?" he asked.

"Yes; but how, sir? You doubtlessly heard that the postilion left as soon as you entered the house."

"Consequently we are without a conveyance; we have paid for our places for nothing, and must remain in this miserable place," said the king, impatiently.

Niclas reddened with anger. "Sir, what right have you to call the town of Grave a miserable place? Believe me, it would be very difficult for you to become a citizen of this miserable place, for you must prove that you have means enough to live in a decent manner, and it appears to me—"

"That we do not possess them," said the king; "vraiment, you are right, our means are very insufficient, and as the inhabitants of Grave will not grant us the rights of citizens, it is better for us to leave immediately. Have, therefore, the goodness to furnish us with the means of doing so."

"There are two ways, an expensive and a cheap one," said Niclas, proudly: "extra post, or the drag-boat. The first is for respectable people, the second for those who have nothing, and are nothing."

"Then the last is for us," said the king, laughing. "Is it not so, brother Henry?—it is best for us to go in the drag-boat."

"That would be best, brother Frederick."

"Have the kindness to call our servant to take the bag, and you, Mr. Niclas, please give us a guide to show us to the canal."

The king took his box and approached the door.

"And my coffee, and the wine," asked Mrs. Niclas, just entering with the drinks.

"We have no time to make use of them, madame," said the king, as he passed her, to leave the room.

But Madame Niclas held him back.

"No time to make use of them," she cried; "but I had to take time to make the coffee, and bring the wine from the cellar."

"Mais, mon Dieu, madame," said the impatient king.

"Mais, mon Dieu, monsieur, vous croyez que je travaillerai pour le roi de Prusse, c'est-a-dire sans paiement."

The king broke out into a hearty laugh, and Balby had to join him, but much against his will.

"Brother Henry," said the king, laughing, "that is a curious way of speaking; 'travailler pour le roi de Prusse,' means here to work for nothing. I beg you to convince this good woman that she has not worked for the King of Prussia, and pay her well. Madame, I have the honor to bid you farewell, and be assured it will always cheer me to think of you, and to recall your charming speech."

The king laughingly took his friend's arm, and nodded kindly to Madame Niclas as he went down the steps.

"I tell you what," said Madame Niclas, as she stood at the door with her husband, watching the departing strangers, who, in company with the guide and their servant, were walking down the street that led to the canal—"I tell you I do not trust those strangers, the little one in particular; he had a very suspicious look."

"But his passport was all right."

"But, nevertheless, all is not right with them. These strangers are disguised princes or robbers, I am fully convinced."

CHAPTER XIII
THE DRAG-BOAT

What a crowd, what noise, what laughing and chatting! How bright and happy these people are who have nothing and are nothing! How gayly they laugh and talk together—with what stoical equanimity they regard the slow motion of the boat! They accept it as an unalterable necessity. How kindly they assist each other; with what natural politeness the men leave the best seats for the women!

The boat is very much crowded. There are a great number of those amiable people who are nothing, and have nothing, moving from place to place cheerily.

The men on the shore who, with the aid of ropes, are pulling the boat, those two-legged horses, groan from exertion. The bagpipe player is making his gayest music, but in vain—he cannot allure the young people to dance; there is no place for dancing, the large deck of the boat is covered with human beings. Old men, and even women, are obliged to stand; the two long benches running down both sides of the boat are filled.

The king enjoyed the scene immensely. The free life about him, the entire indifference to his own person, charmed and delighted him. He leaned against the cabin, by which he was sitting, and regarded the crowd before him. Suddenly he was touched on the shoulder, and not in the gentlest manner. Looking up, he met the discontented face of a peasant, who was speaking violently, but in Dutch, and the king did not understand him; he therefore slightly shrugged his shoulders and remained quiet.

The angry peasant continued to gesticulate, and pointed excitedly at the king and then at a pale young woman who was standing before him, and held two children in her arms.

The king still shrugged his shoulders silently, but when the peasant grasped him for the second time he waved him off, and his eye was so stern that the terrified and astonished peasant stepped back involuntarily.

At this moment a displeased murmur was heard among the crowd, and a number arranged themselves by the side of the peasant, who approached the king with a determined countenance.

The king remained sitting, and looked surprised at the threatening countenances of the people, whose angry words he tried in vain to comprehend.

The still increasing crowd was suddenly separated by two strong arms, and Balby, who had been sitting at the other end of the boat, now approached the king, accompanied by a friend, and placed himself at the king's side.

"Tell me what these men want, mon ami," said Frederick, hastily; "I do not understand Dutch."

"I understand it, sir," said the friend who accompanied Balby, "these people are reproaching you."

"Reproaching me! And why?"

The stranger turned to the peasant who had first spoken, and who now began to make himself heard again in loud and angry tones.

"Monsieur," said the stranger, "these good people are angry with you, and, it appears to me, not entirely without cause. There is a language that is understood without words, its vocabulary is in the heart. Here stands a poor, sick woman, with her twins in her arms. You, monsieur, are the only man seated. These good people think it would be but proper for you to resign your seat."

"This is unheard-of insolence," exclaimed Balby, placing him self determinedly before the king; "let any one dare advance a step farther, and I—"

"Quiet, cher frere, the people are right, and I am ashamed of myself that I did not understand them at once."

He rose and passed through the crowd with a calm, kindly face, and, not appearing to notice them, approached the young woman, who was kneeling, exhausted, on the floor. With a kind, sympathetic smile, he raised her and led her to his seat. There was something so noble and winning in his manner, that those who were so shortly before indignant, were unconsciously touched. A murmur of approval was heard; the rough faces beamed with friendly smiles.

The king did not observe this, he was still occupied with the poor woman, and, while appearing to play with the children, gave each of them a gold piece. But their little hands were not accustomed to carry such treasures, and could not hold them securely. The two gold pieces rolled to the ground, and the ringing noise announced the rich gift of Frederick.

Loud cries of delight were heard, and the men waved their hats in the air. The king reddened, and looked down in confusion.

The peasant, who had first been so violent toward the king, and at whose feet the money had fallen, picked it up and gave it to the children; then, with a loud laugh, he offered his big, rough hand to the king, and said something in a kindly tone.

"The good man is thanking you, sir," said the stranger "He thinks you a clever, good-hearted fellow, and begs you to excuse his uncalled-for violence."

The king answered with a silent bow. He who was accustomed to receive the world's approval as his just tribute, was confused and ashamed at the applause of these poor people.

The king was right in saying he left his royalty on Prussian soil; he really was embarrassed at this publicity, and was glad when Deesen announced that lunch was prepared for him. He gave Balby a nod to follow, and withdrew into the cabin.

"Truly, if every-day life had so many adventures, I do not understand how any one can complain of ennui. Through what varied scenes I have passed to-day!"

"But our adventures arise from the peculiarity of our situation," said Balby. "All these little contretemps are annoying and disagreeable; but seem only amusing to a king in disguise."

"But a disguised king learns many things," said Frederick, smiling; "from to-day, I shall be no longer surprised to hear the police called a hateful institution. Vraiment, its authority and power is vexatious, but necessary. Never speak again of my god-like countenance, or the seal of greatness which the Creator has put upon the brow of princes to distinguish them from the rest of mankind. Mons. Niclas saw nothing great stamped upon my brow; to him I had the face of a criminal—my passport only made an honest man of me. Come, friends, let us refresh ourselves."

While eating, the king chatted pleasantly with Balby of the charming adventures of the day.

"Truly," he said, laughing, as the details of the scene on deck were discussed, "without the interference of that learned Dutchman, the King of Prussia would have been in dangerous and close contact with the respectable peasant. Ah, I did not even thank my protecting angel. Did you speak to him, brother Henry? Where is he from, and what is his name?"

"I do not know, sir; but from his speech and manner he appeared to me to be an amiable and cultivated gentleman."

"Go and invite him to take a piece of pie with us. Tell him Mr. Zoller wishes to thank him for his assistance, and begs the honor of his acquaintance. You see, my friend, I am learning how to be polite, to flatter, and conciliate, as becomes a poor travelling musician. I beg you, choose your words well. Be civil, or he might refuse to come, and I thirst for company."

Balby returned in a few moments, with the stranger.

"Here, my friend," said Balby. "I bring you our deliverer in time of need. He will gladly take his share of the pie."

"And he richly deserves it," said the king, as he greeted the stranger politely. "Truly, monsieur, I am very much indebted to you, and this piece of pie that I have the honor to offer you is but a poor reward for your services. I believe I never saw larger fists than that terrible peasant's; a closer acquaintance with them would have been very disagreeable. I thank you for preventing it."

"Travellers make a variety of acquaintances," said the stranger, laughing, and seating himself on the bench by the king's side, with a familiarity that terrified Balby. "I count you, sir, among the agreeable ones, and I thank you for this privilege."

"I hope you will make the acquaintance of this pie, and find it agreeable," said the king. "Eat, monsieur, and let us chat in the mean while—Henry, why are you standing there so grave and respectful, not daring to be seated? I do not believe this gentleman to be a prince travelling incognito."

"No, sir, take your place," exclaimed the stranger, laughing, "you will not offend etiquette. I give you my word that I am no concealed prince, and no worshipper of princes. I am proud to declare this."

"Ah! you are proud not to be a prince?"

"Certainly, sir."

"It appears to me," said Balby, looking at the king, "that a prince has a great and enviable position."

"But a position, unfortunately, that but few princes know how to fill worthily," said the king, smiling. "Every man who is sufficient for himself is to be envied."

"You speak my thoughts exactly, sir," said the stranger, who had commenced eating his piece of pie with great zeal. "Only the free are happy."

"Are you happy?" asked the king.

"Yes, sir; at least for the moment I am."

"What countryman are you?"

"I am a Swiss, sir."

"A worthy and respectable people. From what part of Switzerland do you come?"

"From the little town of Merges."

"Not far, then, from Lausanne, and the lonely lake of Geneva, not far from Ferney, where the great Voltaire resides, and from whence he darts his scorching, lightning-flashes to-day upon those whom he blessed yesterday. Are you satisfied with your government? Are not your patrician families a little too proud? Are not even the citizens of Berne arrogant and imperious?"

"We have to complain of them, sir, but very rarely."

"Are you now residing in Holland?"

"No, I am travelling," answered the stranger, shortly. He had held for a long time a piece of pie on his fork, trying in vain to put it in his mouth.

The king had not observed this; he had forgotten that kings and princes only have the right to carry on a conversation wholly with questions, and that it did not become Mr. Zoller to be so inquisitive.

"What brought you here?" he asked, hastily.

"To complete my studies, sir," and, with a clouded brow, the stranger laid his fork and pie upon his plate.

But the king's questions flowed on in a continued stream.

"Do you propose to remain here?"

"I believe not, or rather I do not yet know," answered the stranger, with a sarcastic smile, that brought Balby to desperation.

"Are not the various forms of government of Switzerland somewhat confusing in a political point of view?"

"No, for all know that the cantons are free, as they should be."

"Does that not lead to skepticism and indifference?"

The stranger's patience was exhausted; without answering the king, he pushed back his plate and arose from the table.

"Sir, allow me to say that, in consideration of a piece of pie, which you will not even give me time to eat, you ask too many questions."

"You are right, and I beg your pardon," said the king, as he smilingly nodded at Balby to remain quiet. "We travel to improve ourselves, but you have just cause of complaint. I will give you time to eat your piece of pie. Eat, therefore, monsieur, and when you have finished, if it is agreeable, we will chat awhile longer."

When the stranger arose to depart, after an animated and interesting conversation, the king offered him his hand.

"Give me your address," he said, "that is, I beg of you to do so. You say you have not yet chosen a profession; perhaps I may have the opportunity of being useful to you."

The Swiss gave him his card, with many thanks, and returned to the deck.

The king gazed thoughtfully after him.

"That man pleases me, and when I am no longer a poor musician, I shall call him to my side.—Well, brother Henry, what do you think of this man, who, as I see, is named Mr. Le Catt?"

"I find him rather curt," said Balby, "and he appears to be a great republican."

"You mean because he hates princes, and was somewhat rude to me. Concerning the first, you must excuse it in a republican, and I confess that were I in his place I would probably do the same as to the last, he was right to give Mr. Zoller a lesson in manners. Poor Zoller is not yet acquainted with the customs of the common world, and makes all manner of mistakes against bon ton. I believe to-day is not the first time he has been reproved for want of manners."

"Mr. Zoller is every inch a king," said Balby, laughing.

[NOTE.—*The king's conversation with Mr. Le Catt is historical (see Thiebault, vol. 1., p. 218). The king did not forget his travelling adventure, but on his return to Prussia, called Le Catt to court and gave him the position of lecturer, and for twenty years he enjoyed the favor and confidence of the king.*]

CHAPTER XIV
IN AMSTERDAM

Wearied, indeed utterly exhausted, the king and Balby returned to the hotel of the Black Raven, at that time the most celebrated in Amsterdam. They had been wandering about the entire day, examining with never-ceasing interest and delight the treasures of art which the rich patricians of Amsterdam had collected in their princely homes and the public museums. No one supposed that this small man in the brown coat, with dusty shoes and coarse, unadorned hat, could be a king—a king whose fame resounded throughout the whole of Europe. Frederick had enjoyed the great happiness of pursuing his journey and his studies unnoticed and unknown. He had many amusing and romantic adventures; and the joy of being an independent man, of which he had heretofore only dreamed, he was now realizing fully.

The king was compelled now to confess that his freedom and manhood were completely overcome. Hunger had conquered him—hunger! the earthly enemy of all great ideas and exalted feelings. The king was hungry! He was obliged to yield to that physical power which even the rulers of this world must obey, and Balby and himself had returned to the hotel to eat and refresh themselves.

"Now, friend, see that you order something to rejoice and strengthen our humanity," said Frederick, stretching himself comfortably upon the divan. "It is a real pleasure to rue to be hungry and partake of a good meal—a pleasure which the King of Prussia will often envy the Messieurs Zoller. To be hungry and to eat is one of life's rare enjoyments generally denied to kings, and yet," whispered he, thoughtfully, "our whole life is nothing but a never-ceasing hungering and thirsting after happiness, content, and rest. The world alas! gives no repose, no satisfying portion. Brother Henry, let us eat and be joyful; let us even meditate on a good meal as an ardent maiden consecrates her thoughts to a love-poem which she will write in her album in honor of her beloved. Truly there are fools who in the sublimity of their folly wish to appear indifferent to such earthly pleasures, declaring that they are necessary evils, most uncomfortable bodily craving, and nothing more. They are fools who do not understand that eating and drinking is an art, a science, the soul of the soul, the compass of thought and feeling. Dear Balby, order us a costly meal. I wish to be gay and free, light-minded and merry-hearted to-day. In order to promote this we must, before all other things, take care of these earthly bodies and not oppress them with common food."

"We will give them, I hope, the sublimest nourishment which the soil of Holland produces," said Balby, laughing. "You are not aware, M. Frederick Zoller, that we are now in a hotel whose hostess is worshipped, almost glorified, by the good Hollanders."

"And is it this sublime piece of flesh which you propose to place before me?" said the king, with assumed horror. "Will you satisfy the soul of my soul with this Holland beauty? I do not share the enthusiasm of the Hollanders. I shall not worship this woman. I shall find her coarse, old, and ugly."

"But listen, Zoller. These good Dutchmen worship her not be cause of her perishable beauty, but because of a famous pie which she alone in Amsterdam knows how to make."

"Ah, that is better. I begin now to appreciate the Dutchmen, and if the pie is good, I will worship at the same shrine. Did you not remark, brother Henry, that while you stood carried away by your enthusiasm before Rembrandt's picture of the 'Night Watch'—a picture which it grieves me to say I cannot obtain," sighed the king—"these proud Hollanders call it one of their national treasures, and will not sell it—well, did you not see that I was conversing zealously with three or four of those thick, rubicund, comfortable looking mynheers? No doubt you thought we were rapturously discussing the glorious paintings before which we stood, and for this the good Hollanders were rolling their eyes in ecstasy. No, sir; no, sir. We spoke of a pie! They recognized me as a stranger, asked me from whence I came, where we lodged, etc., etc. And when I mentioned the Black Raven, they went off into ecstatic raptures over the venison pasty of Madame von Blaken. They then went on to relate that Madame Blaken was renowned throughout all Holland because of this venison pasty of which she alone had the recipe, and which she prepared always alone and with closed doors. Her portrait is to be seen in all the shop windows, and all the stadtholders dine once a month in the Black Raven to enjoy this pie. Neither through prayers nor entreaties, commands, or threatenings, has Madame Blaken been induced to give up her recipe or even to go to the castle and prepare the pasty. She declares that this is the richest possession of the Black Raven, and all who would be so happy as to enjoy it must partake of it at her table. Balby! Balby! hasten my good fellow, and command the venison pastry," said Frederick, eagerly. "Ah! what bliss to lodge in the Black Raven' Waiter, I say! fly to this exalted woman!"

Balby rushed out to seek the hostess and have himself announced.

Madame Blaken received him in her boudoir, to which she had withdrawn to rest a little after the labors of the day. These labors were ever a victory and added to her fame. There was no better table prepared in Holland than that of the Black Raven. She was in full toilet, having just left the dinner table where she had presided at the table d'hote as lady of the house, and received with dignity the praise of her guests. These encomiums still resounded in her ears, and she reclined upon the divan and listened to their pleasing echo. The door opened and the head waiter announced Mr. Zoller. The countenance of Madame Blaken was dark, and she was upon the point of declining to receive him, but it was too late; the daring Zoller had had the boldness to enter just behind the waiter, and he was now making his most reverential bow to the lady. Madame Blaken returned this greeting with a slight nod of the head, and she regarded the stranger in his cheap and simple toilet with a rather contemptuous smile. She thought to herself that this ordinary man had surely made a mistake in entering her hotel. Neither his rank, fortune, nor celebrity could justify his lodging at the Black Raven. She was resolved to reprove her head waiter for allowing such plain and poor people to enter the best hotel in Amsterdam.

"Sir," said she, in a cold and cutting tone, "you come without doubt to excuse your brother and yourself for not having appeared to-day at my table d'hote. You certainly know that politeness requires that you should dine in the hotel where you lodge. Do not distress yourself, however, sir. I do not feel offended now that I have seen you. I understand fully why you did not dine with me, but sought your modest meal elsewhere. The table d'hote in the Black Raven is the most expensive in Amsterdam, and only wealthy people put their feet under my table and enjoy my dishes."

While she thus spoke, her glance wandered searchingly over Balby, who did not seem to remark it, or to comprehend her significant words.

"Madame," said he, "allow me to remark that we have not dined. My brother, whose will is always mine, prefers taking his dinner in his own apartment, where he has more quiet comfort and can better enjoy your rare viands. He never dines at a table d'hote. In every direction he has heard of your wonderful pie, and I come in his name to ask that you will be so good as to prepare one for his dinner to-day."

Madame Blaken laughed aloud. "Truly said; that is not a bad idea of your brother's. My pasty is celebrated throughout all Holland, and I have generally one ready in case a rich or renowned guest should desire it. But this pie is not for every man!"

"My brother wants it for himself—himself alone," said Balby, decisively. Even the proud hostess felt his tone imposing.

"Sir," said she, after a short pause, "forgive me if I speak plainly to you. You wish to eat one of my renowned pies, and to have it served in a private room, as the General Stadtholder and other high potentates are accustomed to do. Well, I have this morning a pasty made with truffles and Chinese birds'—nests, but you cannot have it! To be frank, it is enormously dear, and I think neither your brother nor yourself could pay for it!"

And now it was Balby's turn to laugh aloud, and he did so with the free, unembarrassed gayety of a man who is sure of his position, and is neither confused nor offended.

Madame Blaken was somewhat provoked by this unrestrained merriment. "You laugh, sir, but I have good reason for supposing you to be poor and unknown. You came covered with dust and on foot to my hotel, accompanied by one servant carrying a small carpet-bag. You have neither equipage, retinue, nor baggage. You receive no visits; and, as it appears, make none. You are always dressed in your simple, modest, rather forlorn-looking brown coats. You have never taken a dinner here, but pass the day abroad, and when you return in the evening you ask for a cup of tea and a few slices of bread and butter. Rich people do not travel in this style, and I therefore have the right to ask if you can afford to pay for my pasty? I do not know who or what you are, nor your brother's position In the world."

"Oh," cried Balby who was highly amused by the candor of the hostess, "my brother has a most distinguished position, I assure you—his fame resounds throughout Germany."

"Bah!" said Madame Blaken, shrugging her shoulders; "the name is entirely unknown to us. Pray, what is your brother, and for what is he celebrated?"

"For his flute," answered Balby, with solemn gravity. Madame Blaken rose and glanced scornfully at Balby. "Are you mating sport of me, sir?" said she, threateningly.

"Not in the least, madame; I am telling you an important truth. My brother is a renowned virtuoso."

"A virtuoso?" repeated the hostess; "I do not understand the word. Pray, what is a virtuoso?"

"A virtuoso, madame, is a musician who makes such music as no other man can make. He gives concerts, and sells the tickets for an enormous price, and the world rushes to hear his music. I assure you, madame, my brother can play so enchantingly that those who hear his flute are forced to dance in spite of themselves. He receives large sums of gold, and if he gives a concert here you will see that all your distinguished people will flock to hear him. You can set your pasty before him without fear—he is able to pay richly for it."

Madame Blaken rose without a word and advanced toward the door. "Come, sir, come. I am going to your brother." Without waiting for an answer, she stepped through the corridor and tapped lightly at the stranger's door. She was on the point of opening it, but Balby caught her hand hastily.

"Madame," said he, "allow me to enter and inquire if you can be received." He wished to draw her back from the door, but the hostess of the Black Raven was not the woman to be withdrawn.

"You wish to ask if I can enter?" repeated she. "I may well claim that privilege in my own house."

With a determined hand she knocked once more upon the door, opened it immediately and entered, followed by Balby, who by signs endeavored to explain and beg pardon for the intrusion.

Frederick did not regard him, his blue eyes were fixed upon the woman who, with laughing good-humor, stepped up to him and held out both of her large, course hands in greeting.

"Sir, I come to convince myself if what your brother said was true."

"Well, madame, what has my brother said?"

"He declares that you can whistle splendidly, and all the world is forced to dance after your music."

"I said play the flute, madame! I said play the flute!" cried Balby, horrified. "Well, flute or whistle," said Madame Blaken, proudly, "it's the same thing. Be so good, sir, as to whistle me something; I will then decide as to the pasty." The king looked at Balby curiously. "Will you have the goodness, brother, to explain madame's meaning, and what she requires of me?"

"Allow me to explain myself," said the hostess. "This gentleman came and ordered a rich pie for you; this pasty has given celebrity to my house. It is true I have one prepared, but I would not send it to you. Would you know why? This is an enormously expensive dish, and I have no reason to believe that you are in a condition to pay for it. I said this to your brother, and I might with truth have told him that I regretted to see him in my hotel—not that you are in yourselves objectionable, on the contrary, you appear to me to be harmless and amiable men, but because of your purses. I fear that you do not know the charges of first-class hotels, and will be amazed at your bill. Your brother, however, assures me that you can afford to pay for all you order; that you make a great deal of money; that you are a virtuoso, give concerts, and sell tickets at the highest price. Now, I will convince myself if you are a great musician and can support yourself. Whistle me something, and I will decide as to the pie."

The king listened to all this with suppressed merriment, and gave Balby a significant look.

"Bring my flute, brother; I will convince madame that I am indeed a virtuoso."

"Let us hear," said Madame Blaken, seating herself upon the sofa from which the king had just arisen.

Frederick made, with indescribable solemnity, a profound bow to the hostess. He placed the flute to his lips and began to play, but not in his accustomed masterly style—not in those mild, floating melodies, those solemn sacred, and exalted strains which it was his custom to draw from his beloved flute. He played a gay and brilliant solo, full of double trills and rhapsodies; it was an astounding medley, which seemed to make a triumphal march over the instrument, overcoming all difficulties. But those soft tones which touched the soul and roused to noble thoughts were wanting; in truth, the melody failed, the music was wanting.

Madame Blaken listened with ever-increasing rapture to this wondrous exercise; these trills, springing from octave to octave, drew forth her loudest applause; she trembled with ecstasy, and as the king closed with a brilliant cadence, she clapped her hands and shouted enthusiastically. She stood up respectfully before the artiste in the simple brown coat, and bowing low, said earnestly:

"Your brother was right, you can surely earn much money by your whistle. You whistle as clearly as my mocking-bird. You shall have the pie—I go to order it at once," and she hastened from the room.

"Well," said the king, laughing, "this was a charming scene, and I thank you for it, brother Henry. It is a proud and happy feeling to know that you can stand upon your feet, or walk alone; in other words, that you can earn a support. Now, if the sun of Prussia sets, I shall not hunger, for I can earn my bread; Madame Blaken assures me of it. But, Henry, did I not play eminently?"

"That was the most glittering, dazzling piece for a concert which I ever heard," said Balby, "and Mr. Zoller may well be proud of it, but I counsel him not to play it before the King of Prussia; he would, in his jealousy, declare it was not music, nothing but sound, and signifying nothing."

"Bravo, my friend," said Frederick, taking his friend's hand; "yes, he would say that. Mr. Zoller played like a true virtuoso, that is to say, without intellect and without soul; he did not make music, only artistic tones. But here comes the pasty, and I shall relish it wondrous well. It is the first meat I have ever earned with my flute. Let us eat, brother Henry."

CHAPTER XV
THE KING WITHOUT SHOES

The pie was really worthy of its reputation, and the king enjoyed it highly. He was gay and talkative, and amused himself in recalling the varied adventures of the past five days.

"They will soon be tempi passati, these giorni felice," he said, sighing. "To-day is the last day of our freedom and happiness; to-morrow we must take up our yoke, and exchange our simple brown coats for dashing uniforms."

"I know one, at least, who is rejoicing," said Balby, laughing, "the unhappy Deesen, who has just sworn most solemnly that he would throw himself in the river if he had to play much longer the part of a servant without livery—a servant of two unknown musicians; and he told me, with tears in his eyes, that not a respectable man in the house would speak to him; that the pretty maids would not even listen to his soft sighs and tender words."

"Dress makes the man," said the king, laughing; "if Deesen wore his cabinet-hussar livery these proud beauties who now despise, would smile insidiously. How strangely the world is constituted! But let us enjoy our freedom while we may. We still have some collections of paintings to examine—here are some splendid pictures of Rembrandt and Rubens to be sold. Then, last of all, I have an important piece of business to transact with the great banker, Witte, on whom I have a draft. You know that Madame Blaken is expensive, and the picture-dealers will not trust our honest faces; we must show them hard cash."

"Does your—Shall I not go to the bankers and draw the money?" said Balby. "Oh no, I find it pleasant to serve myself, to be my own master and servant at the same time. Allow me this rare pleasure for a few hours longer, Balby." The king took his friend's arm, and recommended his search for paintings and treasures to adorn his gallery at Sans-Souci. Everywhere he was received kindly and respectfully, for all recognized them as purchasers, and not idle sight-seers. The dealers appreciated the difference between idle enthusiasm and well-filled purses.

The king understood this well, and on leaving the house of the last rich merchant he breathed more freely, and said:

"I am glad that is over. The rudeness of the postmaster at Grave pleased me better than the civilities of these people. Come, Balby, we have bought pictures enough; now we will only admire them, enjoy without appropriating them. The rich banker, Abramson, is said to have a beautiful collection; we will examine them, and then have our draft cashed."

The banker's splendid house was soon found, and the brothers entered the house boldly, and demanded of the richly-dressed, liveried servant to be conducted to the gallery.

"This is not the regular day," said the servant, with a contemptuous shrug of the shoulders, as he measured the two strangers.

"Not the day! What day?" asked the king, sharply.

"Not the day of general exhibition. You must wait until next Tuesday."

"Impossible, we leave to-morrow. Go to your master and tell him two strangers wish to see his gallery, and beg it may be opened for them."

There was something so haughty and irresistible in the stranger's manner, that the servant not daring to refuse, and still astonished at his own compliance, went to inform his master of the request. He returned in a few moments, and announced that his master would come himself to receive them.

The door opened immediately, and Mr. Abramson stepped into the hall; his face, bright and friendly, darkened when his black eyes fell upon the two strangers standing in the hall.

"You desired to speak to me," he said, in the arrogant tone that the rich Jews are accustomed to use when speaking to unknown and poor people. "What is your wish, sirs?"

The king's brow darkened, and he looked angrily at the supercilious man of fortune, who was standing opposite him, with his head proudly thrown back, and his hands in his pockets. But Frederick's countenance soon cleared, and he said, with perfect composure:

"We wish you to show us your picture-gallery, sir."

The tone in which he spoke was less pleading than commanding, and roused the anger of the easily enraged parvenu.

"Sir, I have a picture-gallery, arranged for my own pleasure and paid for with my own money. I am very willing to show it to all who have not the money to purchase pictures for themselves, and to satisfy the curiosity of strangers, I have set aside a day in each week on which to exhibit my gallery."

"You mean, then, sir, that you will not allow us to enter your museum?" said the king, smilingly, and laying his hand at the same time softly on Balby's arm, to prevent him from speaking.

"I mean that my museum is closed, and—"

A carriage rolled thunderingly to the door; the outer doors of the hall were hastily opened, a liveried servant entered, and stepping immediately to Mr. Abramson, he said:

"Lord Middlestone, of Loudon, asks the honor of seeing your gallery."

The countenance of the Jewish banker beamed with delight.

"Will his excellency have the graciousness to enter? I consider it an honor to show him my poor treasures. My gallery is closed to-day, but for Lord Middlestone, I will open it gladly."

His contemptuous glance met the two poor musicians, who had stepped aside, and were silent witnesses of this scene.

The outer doors of the court were opened noisily, and a small, shrivelled human form, assisted by two servants, staggered into the hall. It was an old man, wrapped in furs; this was his excellency Lord Middlestone. Mr. Abramson met him with a profound bow, and sprang forward to the door that led to the gallery.

Every eye was fixed upon this sad picture of earthly pomp and greatness; all felt the honor to the house of Mr. Abramson. Lord Middlestone, the ambassador of the King of England, desired to see his collection. This was an acknowledgment of merit that delighted the heart of the banker, and added a new splendor to his house.

While the door was being opened to admit his lordship, Balby and the king left the house unnoticed.

The king was angry, and walked silently along for a time; suddenly remaining standing, he gazed steadily at Balby, and broke out into a loud, merry laugh, that startled the passers-by, and made them look wonderingly after him.

"Balby, my friend," he said, still laughing, "I will tell you something amusing. Never in my life did I feel so humble and ashamed as when his excellency entered the gallery so triumphantly, and we slipped away so quietly from the house. Truly, I was fool enough to be angry at first, but I now feel that the scene was irresistibly comic. Oh! oh, Balby! do laugh with me. Think of us, who imagine ourselves to be such splendidly handsome men, being shown the door, and that horrid shrunken, diseased old man being received with such consideration! He smelt like a salve-box, we are odorous with ambrosia; but all in vain, Abramson preferred the salve-box."

"Abramson's olfactories are not those of a courtier," said Balby, "or he would have fainted at the odor of royalty. But truly, this Mr. Abramson is a disgraceful person, and I beg your majesty to avenge Mr. Zoller."

"I shall do so. He deserves punishment; he has insulted me as a man; the king will punish him." [Footnote: *The king kept his word. The Jew heard afterward that it was the king whom he had treated so disrespectfully, and here could never obtain his forgiveness. He was not allowed to negotiate with the Prussian government or banks, and was thus bitterly punished for his misconduct.*]

"And now we will have our check cashed by Mr. Witte. I bet he will not dismiss us so curtly, for my draft is for ten thousand crowns, and he will be respectful—if not to us, to our money."

The worthy and prosperous Madame Witte had just finished dusting and cleaning her state apartment, and was giving it a last artistic survey. She smiled contentedly, and acknowledged that there was nothing more to be done. The mirrors and windows were of transparent brightness—no dust was seen on the silk furniture or the costly ornaments—it was perfect. With a sad sigh Madame Witte left the room and locked the door with almost a feeling of regret. She must deny herself for the next few days her favorite occupation—there was nothing more to dust or clean in the apartment and only in this room was her field of operation—only here did her husband allow her to play the servant. With this exception he required of her to be the lady of the house—the noble wife of the rich banker—and this was a role that pleased the good woman but little. She locked the door with a sigh and drew on her shoes, which she was accustomed always to leave in the hall before entering her state apartment, then stepped carefully on the border of the carpet that covered the hall to another door. At this moment violent ringing was heard at the front door. Madame Witte moved quickly forward to follow the bent of her womanly curiosity and see who desired admittance at this unusual hour. Two strangers had already entered the hall and desired to see the banker.

"Mr. Witte is not at home, and if your business is not too pressing, call again early to-morrow morning."

"But my business is pressing," said Frederick Zoller, hastily, "I must speak with Mr. Witte to-day."

"Can they wish to borrow money from him?" thought Madame Witte, who saw the two strangers through the half-opened door.

"To borrow, or to ask credit, I am sure that is their business."

"May I ask the nature of your business?" said the servant. "In order to bring Mr. Witte from the Casino I must know what you wish of him."

"I desire to have a draft of ten thousand crowns cashed," said Frederick Zoller, sharply.

The door was opened hastily, and Madame Witte stepped forward to greet the stranger and his companion. "Have the kindness, gentlemen, to step in and await my husband; he will be here in a quarter of an hour. Go, Andres, for Mr. Witte." Andres ran off, and Madame Witte accompanied the strangers through the hall. Arrived at the door of the state apartment, she quickly drew off her shoes, and then remained standing, looking expectantly at the strangers.

"Well, madame," said the king, "shall we await Mr. Witte before this door, or will you show us into the next room?"

"Certainly I will; but I am waiting on you."

"On us? And what do you expect of us?"

"What I have done, sirs—to take your shoes off."

The king laughed aloud. "Can no one, then, enter that room with shoes on?"

"Never, sir. It was a custom of my great-grandfather. He had this house built, and never since then has any one entered it with shoes. Please, therefore, take them off."

Balby hastened to comply with her peremptory command. "Madame, it will suffice you for me to follow this custom of your ancestors—you will spare my brother this ceremony."

"And why?" asked Madame Witte, astonished. "His shoes are no cleaner or finer than yours, or those of other men. Have the kindness to take off your shoes also."

"You are right, madame," said the king, seriously. "We must leave off the old man altogether; therefore, you ask but little in requiring us to take off our shoes before entering your state apartment." He stooped to undo the buckles of his shoes, and when Balby wished to assist him, he resisted. "No, no; you shall not loosen my shoes—you are too worthy for that. Madame Witte might think that I am a very assuming person—that I tyrannize over my brother. There, madame, the buckles are undone, and there lie my shoes, and now we are ready to enter your state apartment."

Madame Witte opened the door with cold gravity, and allowed them to pass. "To-morrow I can dust again," she said, gleefully, "for the strangers' clothes are very dirty."

In the mean time, the two strangers awaited the arrival of Mr. Witte. The king enjoyed his comic situation immensely. Balby looked anxiously at the bare feet of the king, and said he should never have submitted to Madame Witte's caprice. The floor was cold, and the king might be taken ill.

"Oh, no," said Frederick, "I do not get sick so easily—my system can stand severer hardships. We should be thankful that we have come off so cheaply, for a rich banker like Witte in Amsterdam, is equal to the Pope in Rome; and I do not think taking off our shoes is paying too dearly to see the pope of Holland. Just think what King Henry IV. had to lay aside before he could see the Pope of Rome—not only his shoes and stockings and a few other articles, but his royalty and majesty. Madame Witte is really for bearing not to require the same costume of us."

The door behind them was opened hastily, and the banker Witte stepped in. He advanced to meet them with a quiet smile, but suddenly checked himself, and gazed with terror at the king.

"My God! his majesty the King of Prussia!" he stammered. "Oh! your majesty! what an undeserved favor you are doing my poor house in honoring it with your presence!"

"You know me, then?" said the king, smiling. "Well, I beg you may not betray my incognito, and cash for Frederick Zoller this draft of ten thousand crowns."

He stepped forward to hand the banker the draft. Mr. Witte uttered a cry of horror, and, wringing his hands, fell upon his knees. He had just seen that the king was barefooted.

"Oh! your majesty! Mercy! mercy!" he pleaded. "Pardon my unhappy wife who could not dream of the crime she was committing. Why did your majesty consent to her insane demand? Why did you not peremptorily refuse to take off your shoes?"

"Why? Well, ma foi, because I wished to spare the King of Prussia a humiliation. I believe Madame Witte would rather have thrown me out of the house than allowed me to enter this sacred room with my shoes on."

"No, your majesty, no. She would—"

At this moment the door opened, and Madame Witte, drawn by the loud voice of her husband, entered the room.

"Wife!" he cried, rising, "come forward; fall on your knees and plead for forgiveness."

"What have I done?" she asked, wonderingly.

"You compelled this gentleman to take off his shoes at the door."

"Well, and what of that?"

"Well," said Mr. Witte, solemnly, as he laid his arm upon his wife's shoulder and tried to force her to her knees, "this is his majesty the King of Prussia!"

But the all-important words had not the expected effect. Madame Witte remained quietly standing, and looked first upon her own bare feet and then curiously at the king.

"Beg the king's pardon for your most unseemly conduct," said Witte.

"Why was it unseemly?" asked his better-half. "Do I not take off my shoes every time I enter this room? The room is mine, and does not belong to the King of Prussia."

Witte raised his hands above his head in despair. The king laughed loudly and heartily.

"You see I was right, sir," he said. "Only obedience could spare the King of Prussia a humiliation. [Footnote: *The king's own words. See Nicolai's "anecdotes of Frederick the Great, "collection V., P.31]* But let us go to your business room and arrange our moneyed affairs. There, madame, I suppose you will allow me to put on my shoes."

Without a word, Mr. Witte rushed from the room for the king's shoes, and hastened to put them, not before the king, but before the door that led into his counting room.

With a gay smile, the king stepped along the border of the carpet to his shoes, and let Balby put them on for him.

"Madame," he said, "I see that you are really mistress in your own house, and that you are obeyed, not from force, but from instinct. God preserve you your strong will and your good husband!"

"Now," said the king, after they had received the money and returned to the hotel, "we must make all our arrangements to return to-morrow morning early—our incognito is over! Mr. Witte promised not to betray us, but his wife is not to be trusted; therefore, by to-morrow morning, the world will know that the King of Prussia is in Amsterdam. Happily, Mr. Witte does not know where I am stopping. I hope to be undisturbed to-day, but by to-morrow this will be impossible."

The king prophesied aright: Madame Witte was zealously engaged in telling her friends the important news that the King of Prussia had visited her husband, and was now in Amsterdam.

The news rolled like an avalanche from house to house, from street to street, and even reached the major's door, who, in spite of the lateness of the hour, called a meeting of the magistrates, and sent policemen to all the hotels to demand a list of the strangers who had arrived during the last few days. In order to greet the king, they must first find him.

Early the next morning, a simple caleche, with two horses, stood at the hotel of the "Black Raven." The brothers Zoller were about to leave Amsterdam, and, to Madame Blaken's astonishment, they not only paid their bill without murmuring, but left a rich douceur for the servants. The hostess stepped to the door to bid them farewell, and nodded kindly as they came down the steps. Their servant followed with the little carpet-bag and the two music-cases.

When Deesen became aware of the presence of the hostess, and the two head-servants, he advanced near to the king.

"Your majesty, may I now speak?" he murmured.

"Not yet," said the king, smiling, "wait until we are in the carriage."

He descended the steps, with a friendly nod to the hostess. Balby and himself left the house.

"See, my friend, how truly I prophesied," he said, as he pointed down the street; "let us get in quickly, it is high time to be off; see the crowd advancing."

Frederick was right; from the end of the street there came a long procession of men, headed by the two mayors, dressed in black robes, trimmed with broad red bands. They were followed by the senators, clothed in the same manner. A great number of the rich aristocrats of the city accompanied them.

Madame Blaken had stepped from the house, and was looking curiously at the approaching crowd, and while she and her maids were wondering what this could mean, the two Mr. Zollers entered the carriage, and their servant had mounted the box. "May I speak now?" said Deesen, turning to the king.

"Yes, speak," said the king, "but quickly, or the crowd will take your secret from you."

"Hostess!" cried Deesen, from the box, "do you know what that crowd means?"

"No," she said, superciliously.

"I will explain; listen, madame. The magistrates are coming to greet the King of Prussia!"

"The King of Prussia!" shrieked the hostess. "Where is the King of Prussia?"

"Here!" cried Deesen, with a malicious grin, as he pointed to the king, "and I am his majesty's cabinet-hussar! Forward, postilion!—quick, forward!"

The postilion whipped his horses, and the carriage dashed by the mayors and senators, who were marching to greet the King of Prussia. They never dreamed that he had just passed mischievously by them.

Two days later, the king and his companions stood on the Prussian border, on the spot where, in the beginning of their journey, the king had written the words "majesty" and "sire."

"Look!" he said, pointing to the ground, "the two fatal words have not vanished away; the sun has hardened the ground, and they are still legible. I must lift them from the sand, and wear them henceforth and forever. Give me your hand, Balby; the poor musician, Frederick Zoller, will bid farewell to his friend, and not only to you, Balby, but farewell also to my youth. This is my last youthful adventure. Now, I shall grow old and cold gracefully. One thing I wish to say before I resume my royalty; confidentially, I am not entirely displeased with the change. It seems to me difficult to fill the role of a common man. Men do not seem to love and trust each other fully; a man avenges himself on an innocent party for the wrongs another has committed. Besides, I do not rightly understand the politenesses of common life, and, therefore, received many reproaches. I believe, on the whole, it is easier to bestow than to receive them. Therefore, I take up my crown willingly."

"Will your majesty allow me a word?" said Deesen, stepping forward.

"Speak, Deesen."

"I thank Mr. Zoller for saving my life. As true as God lives, I should have stifled with rage if I had not told that haughty Hollander who Mr. Zoller was and who I was."

"Now, forward! Farewell, Frederick Zoller! Now I am on Prussian soil, the hour of thoughtless happiness is passed. I fear, Balby, that the solemn duties of life will soon take possession of us. So be it! I accept my destiny—I am again Frederick of Hohenzollern!"

"And I have the honor to be the first to greet your majesty on your own domain," said Balby, as he bowed profoundly before the king.